THE HISTORY OF DRUGS

Alcohol

Other Books in the History of Drugs series:

Alcohol

Ann Manheimer, Book Editor

GREENHAVEN PRESS
An imprint of Thomson Gale, a part of The Thomson Corporation

Detroit • New York • San Francisco • New Haven, Conn. • Waterville, Maine • London

Christine Nasso, *Publisher*
Elizabeth Des Chenes, *Managing Editor*

© 2007 Thomson Gale, a part of The Thomson Corporation.

Thomson and Star logo are trademarks and Gale and Greenhaven Press are registered trademarks used herein under license.

For more information, contact:
Greenhaven Press
27500 Drake Rd.
Farmington Hills, MI 48331-3535
Or you can visit our Internet site at http://www.gale.com

LIBRARY OF CONGRESS CATALOGING-IN-PUBLICATION DATA

Alcohol / Ann Manheimer, book editor.
    p. cm. -- (History of drugs)
    Includes bibliographical references and index.
    ISBN-13: 978-0-7377-2841-5 (hardcover : alk. paper)
    ISBN-10: 0-7377-2841-8 (hardcover : alk. paper)
    1. Alcoholic beverages--History. 2. Alcoholic beverages--Social aspects. 3. Drinking of alcoholic beverages. 4. Drinking customs. I. Manheimer, Ann.
    GT2884.A43 2007
    394.1'2--dc22
                                                          2006022931

Printed in the United States of America
10 9 8 7 6 5 4 3 2 1

Contents

Chapter 1: The Early History of Alcohol

Chapter 2: Alcohol Use in the Twentieth Century

Foreword

Drugs are chemical compounds that affect the functioning of the body and the mind. While the U.S. Food, Drug, and Cosmetic Act defines drugs as substances intended for use in the cure, mitigation, treatment, or prevention of disease, humans have long used drugs for recreational and religious purposes as well as for healing and medicinal purposes. Depending on context, then, the term drug provokes various reactions. In recent years, the widespread problem of substance abuse and addiction has often given the word drug a negative connotation. Nevertheless, drugs have made possible a revolution in the way modern doctors treat disease. The tension arising from the myriad ways drugs can be used is what makes their history so fascinating. Positioned at the intersection of science, anthropology, religion, therapy, sociology, and cultural studies, the history of drugs offers intriguing insights on medical discovery, cultural conflict, and the bright and dark sides of human innovation and experimentation.

Drugs are commonly grouped in three broad categories: over-the-counter drugs, prescription drugs, and illegal drugs. A historical examination of drugs, however, invites students and interested readers to observe the development of these categories and to see how arbitrary and changeable they can be. A particular drug's status is often the result of social and political forces that may not necessarily reflect its medicinal effects or its potential dangers. Marijuana, for example, is currently classified as an illegal Schedule I substance by the U.S. federal government, defining it as a drug with a high potential for abuse and no currently accepted medical use. Yet in 1850 it was included in the U.S. Pharmacopoeia as a medicine, and solutions and tinctures containing cannabis were frequently prescribed for relieving pain and inducing sleep. In the 1930s, after smokable marijuana had gained notoriety as a recreational intoxicant, the Federal Bureau of Narcotics launched a misinformation campaign against the drug, claiming that it commonly induced insanity and murderous violence. While today's medical experts no longer make such claims about marijuana, they continue to disagree about the drug's long-term effects and medicinal potential. Most interestingly, several states have passed medical marijuana initiatives, which allow seriously ill patients compassionate access to the drug under state law—although these patients can still be prosecuted for marijuana use under federal law. Marijuana's illegal status, then, is not as fixed or final as the federal government's current schedule might suggest. Examining marijuana from a historical perspective offers readers the chance to develop a more sophisticated and critically informed view of a controversial and politically charged subject. It also encourages students to learn about aspects of medicine, history, and culture that may receive scant attention in textbooks.

Each book in Greenhaven's The History of Drugs series chronicles a particular substance or group of related drugs—discussing the appearance and earliest use of the drug in initial chapters and more recent and contemporary controversies in later chapters. With the incorporation of both primary and secondary sources written by physicians, anthropologists, psychologists, historians, social analysts, and lawmakers, each anthology provides an engaging panoramic view of its subject. Selections include a variety of readings, including book excerpts, government documents, newspaper editorials, academic articles, and personal narratives. The editors of each volume aim to include accounts of notable incidents, ideas, subcultures, or individuals connected with the drug's history as well as perspectives on the effects, benefits, dangers, and legal status of the drug.

Every volume in the series includes an introductory essay that presents a broad overview of the drug in question. The annotated table of contents and comprehensive index help readers quickly locate material of interest. Each selection is prefaced by a summary of the article that also provides any necessary historical context and biographical information on the author. Several other research aids are also present, including excerpts of supplementary material, a time line of relevant historical events, the U.S. government's current drug schedule, a fact sheet detailing drug effects, and a bibliography of helpful sources.

Greenhaven Press's The History of Drugs series gives readers a unique and informative introduction to an often-ignored facet of scientific and cultural history. The contents of each anthology provide a valuable resource for general readers as well as for students interested in medicine, political science, philosophy, and social studies.

Introduction

Humans have been enjoying alcoholic beverages since before written history began. And they have been worrying about the dangers of alcohol for just as long.

Alcohol was discovered by accident several thousand years ago, when observant people noticed that mixtures of crushed fruits, grains, or honey left open in warm air turned into a drink that created pleasant sensations. They had discovered *fermentation*, in which yeasts turn sugar into alcohol and carbon dioxide; airborne yeasts had landed in the mixtures and fermented them.

Although no one knows exactly when humans started brewing alcoholic beverages on purpose, beer jugs dating from the Stone Age indicate it was at least as long ago as that— around 10,000 B.C. Indeed, humans may have switched from being nomads to being farmers so they could raise grain for beer. The origin of wine making, or viticulture, is more of a mystery; some researchers believe it began around 6000 B.C. with "a barbarous, Early Neolithic people"[1] in Transcaucasia, known now as Armenia, where wine grapes grew wild.

In about 3000 B.C., manufacturing alcohol became a specialized home industry in Sumeria and Egypt, much like baking bread. Beer was the most popular drink; Sumerians drank it through long straws from large clay jugs. Wine was largely reserved for ceremonial and medicinal purposes, although both drinks figured prominently in ancient religion and medicine. In Egypt, Osiris, the god of wine, was worshipped by everyone. Beer, however, was offered more often than wine to the gods, and a portrait of a Sumerian queen drinking with a straw from a jug near her throne suggests that intoxication may even have been part of the governing process. A Sumerian clay table from 2100 B.C. shows beer as the main vehicle for administering medicine.

In China, an early legend attributes the start of wine making to a physician who, in approximately 2500 B.C., fermented rice into medicine for the Yellow Emperor. The importance of the relationship between alcohol and medicine in China can be seen in the fact that the Chinese symbols for the words "alcohol" and "medicine" share the same root, and also in an ancient Chinese proverb: "Alcohol is the best of all medicines."[2]

A Persian legend from roughly 800 B.C. attributes the discovery of alcohol to its healing properties. The story holds that a ruler named Djemshid discovered that grapes packed in jars looked spoiled. Believing them poisonous, he commanded that they be used only for executions. A short time later, a sick girl at the palace tried to commit suicide by eating the forbidden grapes. She fell asleep and awoke cured. Thereafter, Djemshid ordered the grapes to be jarred the same way every year, encouraged everyone to drink the wine, and specifically gave portions to his soldiers to help make them strong.

With alcohol a regular and encouraged part of daily life, it is no wonder that drunkenness occurred among the ancients. Their attitudes toward alcoholic intoxication show both tolerance and concern. Throughout ancient Egypt, for example, temperance was advised but not always observed, as can be seen in an inscription found on a wall in one of the tombs: "His earthly abode was rent and shattered by wine and beer,/ And the spirit escaped before it was called for."[3] Yet an ancient Egyptian calendar includes a day of drunkenness each month. Sumerians seemed generally to treat inebriation lightly, as expressed in the following passage from their poem, *The Epic of Gilgamesh*, describing a man who drank seven goblets of beer: "his spirit was loosened, he became hilarious. His heart became glad and his face shown."[4] Another legend holds that good gods, killed in the battle between good and evil, fell to earth and gave seed to grape vines.

In what may be the first laws governing alcohol, Hammurabi's Code from 1750 B.C. devoted four paragraphs to regulating the prices and measurement of portions, prohibiting unruly gatherings, and prescribing death for tavern keepers who did not turn in known outlaws to authorities. The regulations, however, did not provide any penalty for drunkenness; those first appeared in the Bible's book of Deuteronomy.

In general, biblical writings condemn drunkenness; for example, Noah's leads him to disgrace and Lot's leads to incest. The prophet Hosea quotes Moses saying, "wine and strong drink take away the heart."[5] Nevertheless, the scriptures also frequently praise wine's virtues. Wine drinking in moderation gradually became integrated into Jewish rituals around the sixth century B.C.

In the classical ages, the Greeks were well known for moderation, yet wine played a part in all aspects of life. They typically diluted it with water and followed rules for and praised the virtues of temperance. Nevertheless, drunkenness did become a problem in several Greek city-states. Concern grew with the expansion of those cities and the increasing popularity of the cult of Dionysus, god of wine, whose devotees indulged in wild rites of dancing, sacrifice, and intoxication in their worship of a peasant god of wine and corn as a savior and son of god. In the seventh and sixth centuries B.C., Greeks instituted the first legislation aimed at controlling excessive drinking.

The Romans were also known as moderate drinkers, at least when their city was young. Historians say that Romulus, one of the city's legendary twin founders, "made libations with milk and not with wine,"[6] showing the relative importance of the two beverages. Through the third century B.C., wine was scarce, and laws banned sprinkling wine at funerals as well as any drinking by women, slaves, and men under the age of thirty. However, as climate changes left Italy warmer and drier, viticulture increased. By roughly the second century, Rome's reputation changed; writers criticized its moral deterioration, including the decline of temperance. Dionysian rites spread from Greece to Italy, where they were eventually banned. In the years approaching the end of the era, from roughly 130 to 30 B.C., wine making became a major part of the Roman economy and wine the daily drink in Italy.

Early Christians adopted the Jewish attitude that any problem in the use of wine, which itself was inherently good, was an individual responsibility. Symbolic wine drinking became part of major rituals, and the early Christian church adopted pagan drinking practices in its efforts to attract converts. Unlike pagans, however, Christians believed chronic drunkenness endangered the individual's soul. St. Paul said Christians should not even associate with drunkards and admonished: "It is good neither to eat flesh, nor to drink wine, nor anything whereby thy brother stumbleth or is made weak."[7]

Although people in early history were concerned about the abuse of alcohol, in general, they did not see it as a major social problem. They appreciated the drink's effects and most drinking took place alongside eating in the home. Chronic drunkenness was more a problem of the upper classes who had the time and wealth to engage in it.

The fall of Rome ushered into Europe a period known as the Middle Ages. As urban life declined, the monasteries took on the business of brewing and wine making. For many of the same reasons it had in ancient times, alcohol remained a daily drink in nearly all aspects of life: It was the major thirst quencher in an era of unsafe drinking water; it added nutritional value to poor diets; it was useful as a medicine and anesthetic; and it fostered relief from hard labor and heightened enjoyment at social gatherings. This latter use can be seen, for example, in the eighth-century Anglo-Saxon poem *Beowulf*, which describes the "best of banquets" as one in which "men drank their fill of wine."[8]

Throughout medieval Europe, as during ancient times, drunkenness was primarily associated with occasional festivals and accepted as a part of life. Chronic alcohol abuse remained the province of the upper classes, students, and clerics, who had the time and access to indulge. In general, the only concern over drunkenness for lay people was for the state of their souls—being drunk was not a crime. Laws governing alcoholic beverages were largely designed to protect drinkers and maintain public order.

Probably the most important change in alcoholic beverages during the Middle Ages was the growth of distillation, which turns alcohol into hard liquor, or spirits, such as brandy and whiskey. Although it was probably developed in the Middle East long before the European medieval era, the process did not appear in Europe until the middle of the twelfth century. The practice spread among monks, physicians, and alchemists who used distilled drinks for cures. Initially called *aqua vitae*, or "water of life," the beverages later came to be known as brandy, from the Dutch word *brandewijn*, meaning "burnt wine."

As the Middle Ages gave way to the early modern period, Western society experienced major increases in wealth, population, and technological developments. Perhaps most important, the worldview changed; instead of the medieval focus on the afterlife, society placed more emphasis on the quality of life on earth.

Although attitudes towards alcohol did not change much through the eighteenth century—moderate drinking was accepted, drunkenness was not—the amount of alcohol consumed increased enormously. The sixteenth and seventeenth centuries saw some of the highest rates of consumption in known history; in Sweden, for example, beer consumption in the mid-sixteenth century was roughly forty times the level in the mid-twentieth century. In Denmark, adult workers and sailors drank roughly a gallon a day, the same as the daily ration given to English sailors. It took a while for distilled spirits to become popular; however, after England passed "An Act for the Encouraging of the Distillation of Brandy and Spirits from Corn" in 1690, the annual production of distilled drinks, mostly gin, leapt to nearly one million gallons within four years. This led to the eighteenth-century Gin Craze that resulted in laws discouraging the sale of large quantities of gin. Gin consumption dropped quickly as criticism of drunkenness increased, along with an increase in the consumption of tea and coffee.

The nineteenth century, however, brought major changes in attitudes toward alcohol, as industrialization created the need for a reliable workforce. Self discipline and productivity became more important, piety increased, and drunkenness came to be seen as a threat to efficiency. Urban problems such as crime, poverty, and infant mortality were often blamed on alcohol even though they were probably more the result of overcrowding and unemployment. Temperance groups turned into prohibition groups, calling for a total ban on the production and distribution of alcohol. This movement reached its peak in the United States with the passage of prohibition in 1920, which was repealed a short time later, in 1933.

Alcohol has been a part of human culture throughout history. It has served important roles in religion, diet, medicine, and social interactions. Until relatively recent years, its use in moderation was rarely questioned, and no attempt to ban it outright has ever been successful. The problems of misuse tend to come from a minority of drinkers, yet those problems persist. Particularly in today's world of high-speed freeways and youth culture, alcohol abuse can be devastating. At the same time, health sciences are more aware than ever of the potential benefits of moderate alcohol consumption. Still, societies have not yet developed a balanced approach that allows people to enjoy the benefits of alcohol while preventing the tragedies linked to its abuse.

Notes

1. E. Hyams, *Dionysus: A Social History of the Vine.* New York: Macmillan, 1965, pp. 30–33. Quoted in Gregory A. Austin, *Alcohol in Western Society from Antiquity to 1800: A Chronological History.* Santa Barbara, CA: ABC-Clio, 1985, p. 3.
2. Dwight B. Heath, ed., *International Handbook on Alcohol and Culture.* Westport, CT: Greenwood, 1995, p. 47.
3. Quoted in Austin, *Alcohol in Western Society*, p. 4.
4. Quoted in Austin, *Alcohol in Western Society*, p. 5.
5. Quoted in Austin *Alcohol in Western Society*, p. 13.
6. Quoted in Austin, *Alcohol in Western Society*, p. 17.
7. Quoted in Austin, *Alcohol in Western Society*, p. 35.
8. Quoted in Austin, *Alcohol in Western Society*, p. 56.

The Early History of Alcohol

An Overview of Alcohol Use in Ancient History

David J. Hanson

Stone Age artifacts show that human beings intentionally fermented alcohol as early as 10,000 B.C. In this selection David J. Hanson describes the earliest records of alcohol use by various civilizations, including Stone Age cultures. Hanson explains alcohol's major role in the religion, diet, and health care of these cultures, as well as in releasing tension and increasing social pleasure. He also traces attitudes toward drunkenness in the early cultures of Egypt, China, and Greece, and among early Jews and Christians. David J. Hanson is professor emeritus of sociology at the State University of New York at Potsdam. He has written several books and many chapters on alcohol, including Alcohol Education: What We Must Do; Attitudes, Norms, and Drinking Behavior: A Bibliography; *and* Preventing Alcohol Abuse: Alcohol, Culture, and Control, *from which the following essay is excerpted. He hosts the Web site Alcohol Problems and Solutions (www2.Potsdam.edu/hansondj).*

While no one knows when beverage alcohol was first used, it was presumably the result of a fortuitous accident that occurred at least tens of thousands of years ago. However, the discovery of late Stone Age beer jugs has established the fact that intentionally fermented beverages existed at least as early as the Neolithic period (circa [approximately] 10,000 B.C.), and it has been suggested that beer may have preceded bread as a staple; wine clearly appeared as a finished product in Egyptian pictographs around 4,000 B.C.. The earliest alcoholic beverages may have been made from berries or honey, and wine making may have originated in the wild grape regions of the Middle East. Oral tradition recorded in the Old Testament asserts that Noah planted a vineyard on Mt. Ararat in what is now Turkey. In Sumeria, beer and wine were used for medicinal purposes as early as 2,000 B.C.

Brewing dates from the beginning of civilization in ancient Egypt and alcoholic beverages were very important in that country. Symbolic of this is the fact that while many gods were local or familial, Osiris, the god of wine, was worshiped throughout the entire country. The Egyptians believed that this important god also invented beer, a beverage that was considered a necessity of life; it was brewed in the home "on an everyday basis," [according to researcher Marek Marciniak]. Both beer and wine were deified and offered to gods. Cellars and wine presses even had a god whose hieroglyph was a wine press. The ancient Egyptians made at least seventeen varieties of beer and at least 24 varieties of wine. Alcoholic beverages were used for pleasure, nutrition, medicine, ritual, remuneration and funerary purposes. The latter involved storing the beverages in tombs of the deceased for their use in the afterlife.

Most Ancient People Did Not Regularly Abuse Alcohol

Numerous accounts of the period stressed the importance of moderation, and these norms were both secular and religious. While Egyptians did not generally appear to define inebriety as a problem, they warned against taverns (which were often houses of prostitution) and excessive drinking. After reviewing extensive evidence regarding the widespread but generally moderate use of alcoholic beverages, the historian [William J.] Darby makes a most important observation: all these accounts are warped by the fact that moderate users "were overshadowed by their more boisterous counterparts who added 'color' to history." Thus, the intemperate use of alcohol throughout history receives a disproportionate amount of attention. Those who abuse alcohol cause problems, draw attention to themselves, are highly visible and cause legislation to be enacted. The vast majority of drinkers, who neither experience nor cause difficulties, are not noteworthy. Consequently, moderation is largely ignored by observers and writers.

Beer was the major beverage among the Babylonians, and as early as 2,700 B.C. they worshiped a wine goddess and other wine deities. Babylonians regularly used both beer and wine as offerings to their gods. Around 1,750 B.C., the famous Code of Hammurabi devoted attention to alcohol. However, there were no penalties for drunkenness; in fact, it was not even mentioned. The concern was fair commerce in alcohol. Nevertheless, although it was not a crime, it would appear that the Babylonians were critical of drunkenness.

Alcohol's Spiritual Role in China

A variety of alcoholic beverages have been used in China since prehistoric times. Alcohol was considered a spiritual (mental) food rather than a material (physical) food, and extensive documentary evidence attests to the important role it played in the religious life. [According to writer Zhang Fei-Peng,] "In ancient times people always drank when holding a memorial ceremony, offering sacrifices to gods or their ancestors, pledging resolution before going into battle, celebrating victory, before feuding and official executions, for taking an oath of allegiance, while attending the ceremonies of birth, marriage, reunions, departures, death, and festival banquets."

A Chinese imperial edict of about 1,116 B.C. makes it clear that the use of alcohol in moderation was believed to be prescribed by heaven. Whether or not it was prescribed by heaven, it was clearly beneficial to the treasury. At the time of Marco Polo (1254?–1324?) it was drunk daily and was one of the treasury's biggest sources of income.

Alcoholic beverages were widely used in all segments of Chinese society, were used as a source of inspiration, were important for hospitality, were an antidote for fatigue, and were sometimes misused. Laws against making wine were enacted and repealed forty-one times between 1,100 B.C. and A.D. 1,400. However, a commentator writing around 650 B.C. asserted that people "will not do without beer. To prohibit it and secure total abstinence from it is beyond the power even of sages. Hence, therefore, we have warnings on the abuse of it."

Wine in Ancient Greece

While the art of wine making reached the Hellenic peninsula by about 2,000 B.C., the first alcoholic beverage to obtain widespread popularity in what is now Greece was mead, a fermented beverage made from honey and water. However, by 1,700 B.C., wine making was commonplace, and during the next thousand years wine drinking assumed the same function so commonly found around the world: It was incorporated into religious rituals, it became important in hospitality, it was used for medicinal purposes and it became an integral part of daily meals. As a beverage, it was drunk in many ways: warm and chilled, pure and mixed with water, plain and spiced.

Contemporary writers observed that the Greeks were among the most temperate of ancient peoples. This appears to result from their rules stressing moderate drinking, their praise of temperance, their practice of diluting wine with water, and their avoidance of excess in general. An exception to this ideal of moderation was the cult of Dionysus, in which intoxication was believed to bring people closer to their deity.

Drunks Among the Greeks

While habitual drunkenness was rare, intoxication at banquets and festivals was not unusual. In fact, the symposium, a gathering of men for an evening of conversation, entertainment and drinking typically ended in intoxication. However, while there are no references in ancient Greek literature to mass drunkenness among the Greeks, there are references to it among foreign peoples. By 425 B.C., warnings against intemperance, especially at symposia, appear to become more frequent.

[Ancient Greek writers] Xenophon (431–351 B.C.) and Plato (429–347 B.C.) both praised the moderate use of wine as beneficial to health and happiness, but both were critical of drunkenness, which appears to have become a problem. Hippocrates (cir. 460–370 B.C.) identified numerous medicinal properties of wine, which had long been used for its therapeutic value. Later, both Aristotle (384–322 B.C.) and Zeno [of Citium] (cir. 336–264 B.C.) were very critical of drunkenness.

Alcohol and Jewish Tradition

Among Greeks, the Macedonians viewed intemperance as a sign of masculinity and were well-known for their drunkenness. Their king, Alexander the Great (336–323 B.C.), whose mother adhered to the Dionysian cult, developed a reputation for inebriety.

The Hebrews were reportedly introduced to wine during their captivity in Egypt. When Moses led them to Canaan (Palestine) around 1,200 B.C., they are reported to have regretted leaving behind the wines of Egypt (Numbers 20:5); however, they found vineyards to be plentiful in their new land. Around 850 B.C., the use of wine was criticized by the Rechabites and Nazarites, two conservative nomadic groups who practiced abstinence from alcohol.

In 586 B.C., the Hebrews were conquered by the Babylonians and deported to Babylon. However, in 539 B.C., the Persians captured the city and released the Hebrews from their Exile (Daniel 5: 1–4). Following the Exile, the Hebrews developed Judaism as it is now known, and they can be said to have become Jews. During the next 200 years, sobriety increased and pockets of antagonism to wine disappeared. It became a common beverage for all classes and ages, including the very young; an important source of nourishment; a prominent part in the festivities of the people; a widely appreciated medicine; an essential provision for any fortress; and an important commodity. In short, it came to be seen as a necessary element in the life of the Hebrews. While there was still opposition to excessive drinking, it was no longer assumed that drinking inevitably led to drunkenness. Wine came to be seen as a blessing from God and a symbol of joy (Psalms 104; Zachariah 10:7). These changes in beliefs and behaviors appear to be related to a rejection of belief in pagan gods, a new emphasis on individual morality, and the integration of secular drinking behaviors into religious ceremonies and their subsequent modification. Around 525 B.C., it was ruled that the *kiddush* (pronouncement of the Sabbath) should be recited over a blessed cup of wine. This established the regular drinking of wine in Jewish ceremonies outside the Temple.

Excess Drinking Increases During the Roman Era

King Cyrus of Persia frequently praised to his people the virtue of the moderate consumption of alcohol (cir. 525 B.C.). However, ritual intoxication appears to have been used as an adjunct to decision making and, at least after his death, drunkenness was not uncommon.

Between the founding of Rome in 753 B.C. until the third century B.C., there is consensus among historians that the Romans practiced great moderation in drinking. After the Roman conquest of the Italian peninsula and the rest of the Mediterranean basin (509 to 133 B.C.), the traditional Roman values of temperance, frugality and simplicity were gradually replaced by heavy drinking, ambition, degeneracy and corruption. The Dionysian rites (*Bacchanalia*, in Latin) spread to Italy during this period and were subsequently outlawed by the Senate.

Practices that encouraged excessive drinking included drinking before meals on an empty stomach, inducing vomiting to permit the consumption of more food and wine, and drinking games. The latter included, for example, rapidly consuming as many cups as indicated by a throw of the dice.

By the second and first centuries B.C., intoxication was no longer a rarity, and most prominent men of affairs (for example, Cato the Elder and Julius Caesar) were praised for their moderation in drinking. This would appear to be in response to growing misuse of alcohol in society, because before that time temperance was not singled out for praise as exemplary behavior. As the republic continued to decay, excessive drinking spread and some, such as Marc Antony (d. 30 B.C.), even took pride in their destructive drinking behavior.

Early Christians Encouraged Moderate Use

With the dawn of Christianity and its gradual displacement of the previously dominant religions, the drinking attitudes and behaviors of Europe began to be influenced by the New Testament. The earliest biblical writings after the death of Jesus (circa A.D. 30) contain few references to alcohol. This may have reflected the fact that drunkenness was largely an upper-status vice with which Jesus had little contact. [Writer Gregory A.] Austin has pointed out that Jesus used wine (Matthew 15:11; Luke 7:33–35) and approved of its moderate consumption (Matthew 15:11). On the other hand, he severely attacked drunkenness (Luke 21:34, 12:42; Matthew 24:45–51). The later writings of St. Paul (date 64?) deal with alcohol in detail and are important to Christian doctrine on the subject. He considered wine to be a creation of God and therefore inherently good (1 Timothy 4:4), recommended its use for medicinal purposes (1 Timothy 5:23), but consistently condemned drunkenness (1 Corinthians 3:16–17, 5:11, 6:10; Galatians 5:19–21; Romans 13:3) and recommended abstinence for those who could not control their drinking.

However, late in the second century, several heretical sects rejected alcohol and called for abstinence. By the late fourth and early fifth centuries, the Church responded by asserting that wine was an inherently good gift of God to be used and enjoyed. While individuals may choose not to drink, to despise wine was heresy. The Church advocated its moderate use but rejected excessive or abusive use as a sin. Those individuals who could not drink in moderation were urged to abstain.

It is clear that both the Old and New Testaments are clear and consistent in their condemnation of drunkenness. However, some Christians today argue that whenever "wine" was used by Jesus or praised as a gift of God, it was really grape juice; only when it caused drunkenness was it wine. Thus, they interpret the Bible as asserting that grape juice is good and that drinking it is acceptable to God but that wine is bad and that drinking it is unacceptable. This reasoning appears to be incorrect for at least two reasons. First, neither the Hebrew nor Biblical Greek word for wine can be translated or interpreted as referring to grape juice. Secondly, grape juice would quickly ferment into wine in the warm climate of the Mediterranean region without refrigeration or modern methods of preservation.

The spread of Christianity and of viticulture in Western Europe occurred simultaneously. Interestingly, St. Martin of Tours (316–397) was actively engaged in both spreading the Gospel and planting vineyards.

Judaism Reevaluates Wine

In an effort to maintain traditional Jewish culture against the rise of Christianity, which was converting numerous Jews, detailed rules concerning the use of wine were incorporated into the Talmud. Importantly, wine was integrated into many religious ceremonies in limited quantity. In the social and political upheavals that rose as the fall of Rome approached in the fifth century, concern grew among rabbis that Judaism and its culture were in increasing danger. Consequently, more Talmudic rules were laid down concerning the use of wine. These included the amount of wine that could be drunk on the Sabbath, the way in which wine was to be drunk, the legal status of wine in any way connected with idolatry, and the extent of personal responsibility for behavior while intoxicated.

The Fall of Rome

Roman abuse of alcohol appears to have peaked around mid-first century. Wine had become the most popular beverage, and as Rome attracted a large influx of displaced persons, it was distributed free or at cost. This led to occasional excesses at festivals, victory triumphs and other celebrations, as described by contemporaries. The four emperors who ruled from A.D. 37 to A.D. 69 were all known for their abusive drinking. However, the emperors who followed were known for their temperance, and literary sources suggest that problem drinking decreased substantially in the Empire. Although there continued to be some criticisms of abusive drinking over the next several hundred years, most evidence indicates a decline of such behavior. The fall of Rome and the western Roman Empire occurred in 476.

Around A.D. 230, the Greek scholar Athenaeus wrote extensively on drinking and advocated moderation. The extensive attention to drinking, famous drinks, and drinking cups (of which he described 100) reflected the importance of wine to the Greeks.

Exploring the Beers and Wines of Antiquity

The Economist

The oldest surviving recipe in the world is a recipe for beer found on a thirty-eight-hundred-year-old clay tablet from Sumeria in Mesopotamia. As the Economist *reports in the following selection, beer may be the foundation for all of Western civilization since, according to some research, raising grain for brewing may have been the original motivation for early civilization's switch from a nomadic to an agricultural lifestyle. Beer also played a major role in the ancient Sumerian culture. The* Economist *goes on to describe how beer and wine makers in the United States and Europe try to re-create the tastes of beers and wines drunk in centuries past. The* Economist *is a weekly news and international affairs magazine of the Economist Newspaper Limited in London. Its articles rarely carry bylines of individual authors.*

It may be small—each molecule is less than a billionth of a metre long, and consists of a handful of atoms of carbon, hydrogen and oxygen—but ethyl alcohol makes an excellent time machine. People have enjoyed alcoholic drinks since prehistoric times, making drinking one of the few strands that runs throughout the history of western civilisation. Appreciating the art, music or literature of long-vanished cultures can require years of study; recreating their drinks, and comparing them to what we enjoy today, is simple in comparison, not to mention more fun. The consumption of alcohol is so widespread in history, says Patrick McGovern, an archaeological chemist at the University of Pennsylvania, that drinking is, in effect, "a universal language".

At the same time, of course, different cultures' attitudes to alcohol provide a window on a wide range of social and cultural practices. Alcoholic drinks have always been prized for their supposedly medicinal qualities, though exactly what these qualities were, and how best to take advantage of them, has only become clear in modern times. In short, the drinks of history are familiar enough that we can understand and appreciate them, while different enough to teach us something about the time and place in which they were originally drunk. Some of them can even be re-created at home, with commonly available ingredients.

Beer: The Foundation for Western Civilization

The oldest surviving recipe in the world is for beer. It can be found on a 3,800-year-old clay tablet, as part of a hymn to Ninkasi, the Sumerian goddess of brewing. Sumerian documents, including the legal code drawn up during the reign of King Hammurabi around 1720 B.C., show that beer played an important role in Mesopotamian rituals, myths and medical practices. It was drunk by all members of society, from top to bottom, and tavern keepers were expected to abide by strict rules: the penalty for overcharging, for example, was drowning.

In addition to being at the heart of Mesopotamian culture, beer may even have been the foundation for the whole of western civilisation. In the 1950s Jonathan Sauer, an American botanist, suggested that the original motivation for domesticating cereal crops (and thus switching from a nomadic to a settled lifestyle) might have been to make beer, rather than bread. The question of whether beer or bread came first has been debated ever since.

Supporters of Sauer's idea have pointed out that many of the first cereals to be farmed were unsuitable for baking without tiresome preparation, but were suitable for brewing. Beer, they suggest, may have emerged in an attempt to make wild barley edible by mixing it with water and fruit. The thick beer produced in this way would be just as nutritious as bread, in addition to being slightly alcoholic.

Sumerian Beer

Sumerian documents lend credence to this idea. For although Sumerian beer was made using *bappir*, a form of bread that could be stored for long periods, it seems that bappir was consumed only when no other food was available. In other words, its primary function may have been to store the raw materials for making beer in a convenient form.

If beer really does underpin western civilisation, that would explain its high status in Sumerian culture. The seal of Lady Pu-Abi, queen of the city of Ur around 2600 B.C., shows her drinking beer from a cup through a straw; just such a straw, made of gold and lapis lazuli, was found in her tomb, and can be seen today in the British Museum.

So what would this Ur-beer have tasted like? A number of attempts have been made to brew Sumerian beer according to the Ninkasi recipe. Two such tipples were made in the early 1990s at the Anchor Brewery in San Francisco, though they were not put on sale to the general public. They involved a certain amount of guesswork. One problem, says Michael Jackson, a beer expert who has tasted various pseudo-Sumerian beers over the years, is that modern brewers avoid the use of wild yeast, which would have made the original beers taste "winey and sour". Another problem, he says, is that it is not clear what was added to ancient beers to balance the taste of the grain. It may well have been fruit, but could also have been honey.

This means there are various modern beers that may resemble the ancient kind. Mr Jackson notes that lambic beers from Belgium use wild yeast, for example; he also recommends Sahti, a Finnish beer that is flavoured with juniper, which he describes as "the last primitive beer to survive in Europe". Philip Rogers, of the Anchor Brewing Company, says that the Ninkasi brew he tasted was reminiscent of mead; another beer, also based on the Ninkasi recipe, has been compared to Jade, a French organic beer.

Cocktails from 700 B.C.

To further complicate matters, says Mr McGovern, the distinction between beer, wine and mead starts to break down once honey and fruit are included in the brewing process. Furthermore, his analysis of drinking vessels, found in a tomb in central Turkey dating to around 700 B.C. and thought to be that of King Midas, suggests that beer, wine and mead may have been mixed together in equal quantities to make an early form of cocktail.

A similar drink seems to have been adopted by the Minoan civilisation of Crete after about 1500 B.C. Mr McGovern is currently collaborating with a Cretan wine maker to recreate this drink: six different blends of wine, spices, mead and beer are brewing at this very moment [December 2001]. His findings have also been used by Sam Calagione of the Dogfish Head Craft Brewery in Lewes, Delaware, to create a beer called "Midas Touch", which was launched in June [2001]. . . .

Galen's Wine: Rome, circa A.D. 170

Some time towards the end of the second century A.D., Galen of Pergamum, physician to the [Roman] emperor Marcus Aurelius, descended into the Palatine cellars in Rome and conducted what must be regarded as one of the greatest vertical wine-tastings in history. Before his appointment as imperial physician, Galen had been a doctor at a gladiatorial school, where he had learned of the medical value of wine to disinfect wounds. Galen also believed that wine was an extremely potent medicine. So when it came to preparing a theriac, or medicinal potion for the emperor, Galen decided that it should be based on the finest wine in the world. "Since all that is best from every part of the earth finds its way to the great ones of the earth," he wrote, "from their excellence must be chosen the very best for the greatest of them all." He duly headed for the cellars.

In Roman times, it was universally agreed that the finest wine was that of the Falernian region near Naples. In fact, in a foreshadowing of the French *appellation* regulations [governing labeling wine by geographical region], there were three types of Falernian wine. Caucinian Falernian originated from vineyards on the highest slopes of Mount Falernus; Faustian Falernian came from vineyards on the central slopes; and wine from the lower slopes was known simply as Falernian.

Perhaps surprisingly, given modern tastes, the most prized Falernian was a white wine. Roman sources indicate that the grapes were picked fairly late, resulting in a heavy, sweet wine that was golden in colour and could be aged for decades. The nearest contemporary equivalents would appear to be long-aged sauternes wines, such as Chateau d'Yquem [a famous French vineyard]. But Falernian would have tasted very different, for a number of reasons. For a start, it was allowed to maderise [to heat and change flavour], which caused it to turn amber or brown. A modern drinker presented with a glass of Roman wine might also notice that its taste was affected by the pitch or resin that was used to make impermeable the earthenware jars in which the wine was stored.

But the most dramatic difference between Roman and modern wine is that the Romans never drank wine on its own; they always mixed it with other ingredients. Indeed, the practice of drinking wine straight was regarded as barbaric. Most often, wine was simply diluted. The amount of water added depended on the circumstances (it was up to the host to decide) and the temperature, but the proportions were typically one part wine to three parts water. Diluting wine served two purposes: it made it into a thirst-quenching drink that could be consumed in large quantities, and the presence of alcohol also made the water safe to drink, an important consideration in the growing cities of the Roman Empire, as it still was in 18th-century Europe.

On occasion, wine was diluted with seawater. According to Pliny the Elder, one of several Roman authorities on wine, this was done "to enliven the wine's smoothness". But water was not the only additive. Snow was sometimes mixed with wine to cool it; honey was sometimes added to create an aperitif known as *mulsum*; and various herbs and spices were commonly added to wine to mask the fact that it had turned to vinegar. Keeping wine in good condition was difficult in Roman times, so most wine was drunk within a year of production; "old" wine was categorised as wine more than a year old.

Rome's Finest

As a wine-lover, Galen must have relished the prospect of searching the imperial cellars for the finest Falernian. He started with 20-year-old Falernian and then tasted earlier and earlier vintages. "I kept on until I found a wine without a trace of bitterness. An ancient wine which has not lost its sweetness is the best of all." Eventually, Galen settled on a Faustian Falernian as the finest wine in existence. Alas, he did not record the year. Earlier in the Roman period, the general consensus had been that the Falernian of 121 B.C. was the best vintage; according to Pliny, this wine was still being drunk 160 years later, when it was offered to Caligula. So it seems likely that Galen would have had Falernian vintages as much as 200 years old available during his tasting session.

But while Falernian was the finest Roman wine, it was hardly typical of what Romans like Galen drank every day. How can such wines be re-created? Hervé Durand, a French wine maker, has set up a "Roman vineyard" near Nîmes in the south of France, where he follows the wine-making proce-

Making Wine in Ancient Times

Grape wine, called *tin* or *gestin* in Mesopotamia and *irp* in Egypt, has an alcohol content of 8–14% by volume. The wild grape sub-species *Vitis vinifera sylvestris* was the source of almost all ancient wine and was likely domesticated in Mesopotamia and the Levant by at least the fifth millennium B.C. *V. vinifera*'s resistance to disease and cold, its high natural acidity, and its high sugar content made the species ideal for alcohol production. Wine was commonly served in large quantities in ancient Egypt and Mesopotamia. Wine was a symbol of power and status in these societies and tended to be used in feasts that signaled social differences.

The techniques used to make wine in the ancient Near East were similar in broad outline to the ones used by vintners today. Grape vines required constant attention among other activities, trellises were built and maintained, grazing animals were kept at bay, dormant vines were pruned, and plants were watered. All of this work had to be done throughout the life of a vine even though the plant did not produce grapes usable for wine production during its first three to five years of life. When grapes were harvestable, workers picked the fruits, often by hand or with a sharp blade or stone, and put them in baskets that were carried to a treading area.

A two-step process was used to extract the juice from the grapes. First, the grapes were thrown into vats and crushed by workers walking barefoot over them. The juice flowed into pottery containers through holes near the bottom of the vats; depictions from Old Kingdom Egypt do not show these containers. The second stage in the pressing process was designed to capture the remaining juices from the treaded grapes. The treaded grapes, including stems, seeds, and skins, were placed in a sack. Workers twisted either the two ends of the sack, poles tied to the sides of the sack, or one side of the sack with the other side tied to a fixed pole to press the remaining juice out of the mixture. The juice that was extracted at this second stage was either added to the juice from the treading or fermented separately.

"Drinking Beer in a Blissful Mood: Alcohol Production, Operational Chains, and Feasting in the Ancient World," Justin Jennings et al., Current Anthropology 46.2 (April 2005), p. 275.

dures described by Roman writers as closely as possible. He produces three pseudo-Roman wines: Turriculae, a white wine that is lightly flavoured with salt water; Carenum, a spiced red wine; and Mulsum, which is flavoured with honey. Similarly, several wine makers in Italy make wines that trade on the Roman connection. But they are not designed to be diluted or mixed with honey and they are not full of herbs. In other words, they are quite palatable, and thus, alas, not authentic.

According to Jerry Paterson, an expert on Roman wine at the University of Newcastle-upon-Tyne in England, the contemporary wines that are most similar to Roman wines are young, sweet white wines, such as those made in Germany or around the French town of Vouvray. The nearest red wine, he suggests, is Italian wine made with the Aglianico grape. Add half a cup of honey to a bottle of white wine, and refrigerate, to make *mulsum*; or simply add water in order to drink wine, Roman style.

Sir Francis Drake's Booty

On the afternoon of April 19th, 1587, Sir Francis Drake led his convoy of 31 ships into the port of Cadiz, where the Spanish navy was being prepared to invade England. The Spanish were taken completely by surprise, and Drake's men quickly looted, sank or burnt every ship in sight. After clearing the harbour of stores and fending off a Spanish attack, Drake and his ships escaped without the loss of a single man. Back in England, Drake became a national hero, and his daring attack became known as the "singeing of the King of Spain's beard".

As well as setting back the Spanish plan to invade England by several months, Drake's daring attack sealed the success of a popular new drink. For among the stores that he plundered from Cadiz were 2,900 large barrels of sack, a wine made in the Jerez region of Spain, and the forerunner of today's sherry. Its popularity stemmed from a law, passed in 1491, that wines made for export should be exempt from taxes. (The name sack is derived from the Spanish word *sacar*, meaning to take out, or export.) The wine makers of Jerez looked for overseas markets, and sack started to take off in England. In 1587, the celebratory drinking of the sack brought back from Cadiz by Drake gave it a further boost and made it hugely fashionable, notwithstanding its Spanish origin.

For obscure chemical reasons, sack was an unusually long-lasting and robust wine. This made it ideal for taking on long sea voyages, during which alcoholic drinks acted as a vital social lubricant that lessened the hardship of spending weeks packed into a cramped ship. Columbus took sack with him to the new world in the 1490s, making it the first wine to be introduced into the Americas. When Magellan set out to circumnavigate the world in 1519 he spent more on sack than he did on weapons.

The Bard Sings Sack's Praises

But it was in England that sack was most popular. By far the most famous tribute to it was written by William Shakespeare in 1598. In "Henry IV, Part 2", Falstaff sings its praises in a long speech and concludes: "If I had a thousand sons, the first human principle I would teach them should be, to forswear thin potations and to addict themselves to sack." This was, of course, an anachronism: the play was set long before sack was introduced to England. But it is tempting to conclude that Falstaff's words reflect Shakespeare's own love of sack, which was widely shared. His fellow playwrights Ben Jonson and Christopher Marlowe also wrote hymns to sack; Marlowe was probably drinking it on the night he was killed in a tavern brawl.

In 1604, sack was granted official recognition of sorts when James I issued an ordinance limiting its consumption at court. "We[,] considering that oftentimes sundry of our nobility and others, dieted and lodged in our Court, may for their better health desire to have Sacke, our pleasure is that there be allowed to the sergeant of our cellar twelve gallons of Sacke a day, and no more." By this time sack was popularly known as sherris-sack (sherris being a corruption of Jerez), which eventually became the modern word *sherry*.

Sack was still popular in the late 17th century, and appears frequently in the diary of [British diarist] Samuel Pepys. On the morning of March 5th 1668, Pepys was summoned to Westminster to defend the Navy Office's practice of paying sailors with negotiable bills instead of money. On the way he decided to fortify himself: "to comfort myself did go to the Dog and drink half-a-pint of mulled sack". Pepys also refers several times to "sack-posset", a medicinal brew of sack, sugar, spices, milk and beaten eggs that was traditionally served at weddings in early colonial America.

A Glass from the Past

What did sack taste like, and can its taste be experienced today? For many years it was believed that sack derived its name from *seco*, meaning dry, and that it was therefore a dry wine. But according to Julian Jeffs, an expert on the history of sherry, this is wrong, and sack was actually sweet. It was not aged for more than a year or two, unlike modern sherry, which is usually aged for at least three years. This suggests, says Mr Jeffs, that sack probably tasted quite similar to a cheap, young oloroso [dry] sherry. It was often further sweetened with honey or sugar: hence Falstaff's nickname of "Sir John Sack-and-sugar".

Re-creating the drinks of the past is an intellectual challenge, says Mr McGovern. It is an inexact science, and the results can be horrible. "But once you've created something that's tasty and delicious, it's like you've brought the past back to life," he says. "It makes it much more real for people—it isn't just something forever buried." Better still, in addition to re-creating a tiny aspect of the past, there is now strong scientific evidence that alcohol, taken in moderation, can help you travel forward in time too, by reducing the risk of heart disease by as much as 40%.

Drinking Patterns of Ancient Egypt

Abdel Monheim Ashour

Thousands of years before Christ, beer and bread were an essential part of the Egyptian diet; in fact, beer was considered more a food than a drink. In this review of alcohol in Egyptian history, Abdel Monheim Ashour describes how Egyptian drinking patterns evolved through the centuries alongside religious practices. As various invading cultures brought different kinds of worship that included the use of wine, and as improvements in technology permitted wine to be stored for longer periods, Egyptian tastes broadened. However, Ashour writes, partly in reaction to the historic succession of foreign rulers and partly in reaction to Western culture, Egyptians have always practiced moderation in drinking alcoholic beverages. Abdel Monheim Ashour is a professor of psychiatry and gerontology and head of the Department of Psychogeriatric Research at Ain Shams University in Egypt. He is also the founder of the International Psychogeriatric Association.

Egyptian drinking is unique. The drinking pattern and the overall consumption of alcohol have remained stable for over 4,000 years. It is hypothesized that culture and religion were the major determinants of this behavior. Egyptian religion and culture, including drinking, changed little over all these years.

The hallmark of Egyptian drinking is very low consumption. Alcohol was available most of the time, but demand was modest most of the time. Egyptians were essentially drinkers of grain-based beer. They treated the different alcoholic bever-

Abdel Monheim Ashour, *International Handbook on Alcohol and Culture*, edited by Dwight B. Heath, Westport, CT: Praeger, 1995. Copyright © 1995 by Dwight B. Heath. All rights reserved. Reproduced by permission of Greenwood Publishing Group Inc., Westport, CT.

ages differently. Beer was the everyday food and beverage for everyman. Wine was the drink of episodic festivities. [Distilled] spirits were (and are) thought to be evil and better avoided.

Egyptian history is unique in the fact that it is highly reliable, being overwhelmingly documented over the last 7,000 years. Carvings or paintings on walls, papyri, and other relics reveal many details of earlier Egyptian life.

Predynastic and Early Dynastic Drinking

As early as the Predynastic period in Egyptian history (before 3200 B.C.), Egyptians (in both the north and south) had developed a specific belief in the continuation of life after death. This afterlife was envisaged as similar to existence before death. The deceased were provided with the requirements for continued existence, including food and drink.

There were many deities. Priests performed acts of worship before the gods, with offerings of food, drink, and clothing thrice a day. During the First through Fourth Dynasties, burial customs became more elaborate, including special rooms to store food and drink. Funerary temples were built to hold ever-increasing amounts of such offerings. There were many attempts (not limited to the famous) to preserve the body with a lifelike appearance, to help the spirit partake of the food and drink.

Beer Is Sustenance

Egypt developed into a highly organized and centralized theocracy. The divine king was viewed as the son of the sun and mediator between gods and humankind. The people were under his strict control. No cult rivaled that of Re (the Sun Cult) in power and importance, and solar temples were constructed. Religion was organized for the benefit of the king and the state. An ethical code had already been developed by Egyptians, supposedly with a divine authorization, and codified in the literature. Only the king could hope to achieve an eternal existence. Vicarious eternity was the religious incentive for people who participated by contributing labor or offerings in support of the vast mortuary complexes that surrounded the pyramids.

The drinking patterns of Egyptians in the Old Kingdom [3150–2350 B.C.] fit well into this culture and religion. In simplest terms, Egyptians in the Old Kingdom saw bread and beer as basic to their sustenance; wine and spirits were still thought to be dangerous.

Beer and bread were inseparable, to the degree that beer was perceived more as a food than as an alcoholic beverage. This notion still survives. Bread and beer, both as food and as offerings, were the focus of many social and cultural activities. They were offered twice daily in the funerary temples to the dead god-king, and were consumed by the staffs of such temples, who could number as many as 300 persons. The Egyptian workman's packed lunch usually consisted of bread, beer, and onions. Children and nursing mothers drank beer for health and nutritional reasons. When guests arrived at the door of a host holding a party, the host would greet them with the phrase "Bread and beer" (the equivalent of "hello!"). Most beer-drinking was moderate and social. Yet there were also times and places for getting drunk through excessive drinking. A notorious example of this is the excessive drinking by mourners on the last day of mourning (forty or seventy days after the death). Mourners consumed on that single day what they normally consumed in a whole month. Excessive beer-drinking took place at rich men's parties. It was even hailed in poetry.

Meanwhile, there were warnings against and stigmatization for frequenting beer houses and abusing beer and wine. Beer was home-brewed and also made in special breweries for offerings. Wheat and barley were local products, and so was the storage pottery. Bread was often included in the process of brewing; the beer was thick, nutritious, and had to be consumed fresh. The pottery containers were of porous clay suitable for short-term storage only. This type of beer still exists in Nubia and Sudan, and is called *bouza*. Wine and liqueurs were made from figs, palm dates, and grapes. Because of the considerable loss through evaporation and seepage, most Egyptian wines were probably drunk young.

In the Old Kingdom, religious and cultural rituals were not gestures of piety toward the gods (a sentiment that became common in the New Kingdom) but a self-imposed duty, a gratification, and a familiar and recognized pattern of behavior. In the Old Kingdom, people were confident, hardworking, and optimistic. When they died and were buried with the necessary provisions for the hereafter, it was expected that they would go to the "godly West" and live again, exactly as on earth. This morality and religion were behind the rather liberal use of beer in that period.

A Changing Society

The First Intermediate Period consisted of the Ninth and Tenth Dynasties. It was a society collapsing from within. The very people who had so wished to prolong the joys of life beyond death now questioned the values of their lives and their society.

The Middle Kingdom (Eleventh and Twelfth) Dynasties, restored stability to Egypt. The omnipotence of Re was replaced by the cult of Osiris (god of land and of grain) and other deities. The ordinary person came to expect an afterlife that was no longer dependent upon the king's favor but could be achieved through the performance of the correct ritual and burial procedures and through devoted worship of Osiris. Every Egyptian believed that upon death he or she was required to face trial before a tribunal of judges. There was an increasing emphasis placed on moral fitness as a hope for individual immortality. The Middle Kingdom was essentially the period when Eyptians of all classes first sought individual eternity and aspired to it through moral righteousness in life.

The New Kingdom (1600 B.C.–330 B.C.): Drink and Religion Increase

The Middle Kingdom came to an end with the Hyksos [a group of Southwest Asiatic or Semitic people of mixed ethnicity] invasion at the end of the Thirteenth Dynasty. The Hyksos were finally driven out, and the New Kingdom was established with the Eighteenth Dynasty. Its princes (from around Thebes) attributed their ascendancy to support of the local god Amun (air god). They then associated this local god with the old solar god, Re, creating the omnipotent Amun-Re (king of the gods).

There were two types of temples: for the gods and for the dead. There also were two groups of temple rituals. The daily ritual in both cult and mortuary temples provided a dramatization of commonplace events in everyday existence. A second group of rituals were the festivals at regular (often yearly) intervals, the main event being the god's procession. Such festivals attracted huge numbers of pilgrims.

Large quantities of beer were consumed in the daily temple ritual, and much beer and wine was consumed in the temple festivals. Improved technology was available to keep wine for longer periods (e.g., filtering, boiling, and use of storage vessels made of stone).

A festival could last as long as a month, as did Amun's festival at Opet [celebrating the benevolent hippopotamus goddess]. The increased religious activity in the New Kingdom was associated with material abundance and prosperity. The new cult of Aten (god of the entire kingdom) does not seem to have provided much of a moral philosophy. Once more we can see why much alcohol was consumed. It was in the New Kingdom that two wise men, Ani and Amenehotep, wrote works discouraging students from excessive drinking either at home or at inns. They described symptoms we would now call alcoholism, alcohol-related personality deterioration, and death.

Greco-Roman Egypt (330 B.C.–A.D. 150)

The Egyptian and Greek cults of the Ptolemies [Greek rulers of Egypt] were distinct, but they were both directed to the same monarchs, and as gods the Ptolemies shared the temples of Egyptian deities. Thus the ruler cult was a cement binding together the heterogeneous elements that made up the population of Egypt.

It appears that even the Jews, as refugees in Egypt, stranded in a world of Hellenistic paganism, were apt to stray from the narrow path of strict observance, and to become in some degree hellenized. There is no evidence that the religion of the Roman conquerers produced any appreciable effect on the religious life in Egypt. There was no decay in Egyptian religion but a new orientation of religious consciousness. There was a movement away from the old communal cults and toward a more personal relationship to the deity. There was also a re-emergence of Osiris and Horus [god of light], associated with a general revival of Egyptian sentiment.

The religion of Roman Egypt was a composite of many strands. At its best, it was a noble monotheism, but it also embraced magic and theurgy. Its points of resemblance to Christianity are obvious. The Romans had the policy of letting the Egyptians continue their way of life and their own language, which was Coptic. We can safely say that drinking habits of the Egyptians outside of Greek-dominated cities in the Greco-Roman period differed little from those of the previous 3,000 years.

The Christian Triumph (150–640): Drinking Decreases

There is no satisfactory direct evidence for the existence of Christian communities in Egypt during the first century. By the end of the second century, Christianity must have been fairly widespread even in Upper Egypt. The atmosphere of the time was favorable to its spread. For the more educated, the way had been prepared by its monotheism, its high moral standards, its redemptive and sacramental mysteries, and its hope of immortality. Simpler folk found a bridge in the popular worship of Osiris as the god of resurrection. Egyptian Christians took much of their pagan outlook with them into their new creed (e.g., food and wine in tombs, preservation of bodies after death, and other, gnostic elements). Egypt's other great contribution was monasticism.

From around 350, we are justified in regarding Egypt as broadly a Christian country. The Christian triumph was no accident. Christianity was a more sophisticated religion for which paganism had paved the way. The Egyptian Christians, the Copts, still appoint their own patriarch of Alexandria and follow their own interpretation of the Scriptures. They regard theirs as the Orthodox Church that held firm to the Nicene Creed [from the Christian ecumenical council of A.D. 325].

The stand of Coptic Christianity on alcoholic beverages and drinking is multifaceted. The word "wine" appears in different concrete and symbolic contexts in the Bible. The Old Testament describes wine as a gift of God to believers, short of getting drunk. Wine is part of the offerings in certain festivals. There is much condemnation of drunkenness. The conversion of water into wine by Jesus is meant to be a symbolic miracle rather than an exhortation to consume wine. Jesus is never explicitly reported as having drunk wine (although we presume, on the basis of context, that he did). Jesus uses wine as a symbol for his blood, according to Coptic Christians, because both are extracted, by squeezing. St. Paul advocates wine as medicine only for a case of edema in a person who was hurt by drinking too much water. Yet Paul repeatedly speaks against drinking, demonstrating physical and social ailments caused by it. The concluding compromise in face of these controversial biblical stands on wine, as summarized by the Orthodox Coptic Church, is the following: drinking small amounts of fresh wine is allowed, but excessive wine-drinking and drinking any amount of spirits are banned. Although we have no access to documents, we can safely say that Coptic Christianity must have discouraged much drinking, especially of spirits.

Drinking Under Arab Rule

Egypt was conquered by the Arabs in 641. The conversion of the bulk of the Egyptian population to the Muslim faith was slow. Arabization and Islamization took several centuries. Historians of this period tell us little about the common people, but it is frequently reiterated that invaders like the Shiite Fatimids did not try to impose their beliefs on the population. The Coptic Church flourished during the Fatimid period (969–1171).

One can safely assume that the Egyptians' culture and habits, including their mild drinking behavior, were rather stable over centuries. To be sure, the enigmatic if not eccentric Caliph [spiritual leader] Al-Hakim did impose a form of prohibition, and poured beer and wine into the Nile, along with honey. His prohibition was short-lived; he disappeared and his body was never found. Another example to show that the unique Egyptian culture survived regardless of who sat on the throne is the case of the Mamluk Empire (1382–1517). Mamluks, who were nominally Muslims, frequently behaved like pagans. During the Ottoman age (1516–1805), Egypt was relegated to the status of a province within a larger empire that was uniform in religion but varied in language and ethnicity. The alienation between rulers and ruled continued.

Searching in Maccarese's (1436) book on Cairo, I found some anecdotal mention of alcohol in Egyptian life in those days. Because the weather was warm and humid, wines did not keep, so Egyptians learned to add molasses or honey as a preservative. Less beer was consumed. Wine was made only in the early autumn.

Many Christians believe that their religion forbids them to get drunk. They do not drink at all during fast days. Although the Coptic Christian minority was more affluent, their drinking was never excessive. Muslims, who occasionally participated in riots against the churches during the Mamluk regime, looted the sacramental wines together with other items from the churches. Looters are often described as having consumed the wine and fallen drunk in the streets.

Nineteenth- and Twentieth-Century Egypt

[Turkish viceroy] Mohamed Ali's modernization campaign expanded agriculture for export, introduced industrialization, and suffered military expansion. A cash-crop economy and changes in land tenure altered agricultural production from grain and fruit to cotton and sugarcane. The *fallah* (peasant, or small-scale farmer) worked 250 days a year on irrigated land and also was expected to provide labor in lieu of paying taxes. The army was feared and the factories were disliked. Aliens manned the army, and Egyptians could not call their land their own. Some Egyptianization of government was started, but it took a century to make a difference. Unfortunately for Egypt, none of Mohamed Ali's successors had his energy, imagination, or political skills. The Suez Canal shares were lost to foreigners, who were granted increasing power as a result of concessions. The British protectorate meant that the English were the real rulers in Egypt from 1881 to 1954. [British] Governor [Lord] Cromer dissolved what industry there was and transformed diversified farming into monoculture, abandoning food for cotton to feed the mills of Lancashire [England]. Banditry appeared in rural areas. Throughout World War I, Egyptians suffered from inflation. All social problems in Egypt had been shelved by successive governments with the excuse that they had more important matters to worry about, notably negotiating a treaty with England. Egypt was granted independence in 1923 but under a royal family, whom many Egyptians viewed as alien interlopers imposed from without. A fundamentalist religious revival occurred in the early 1900s, which brought an alternative to the constant bickering of political parties over power.

The modern Egyptian problems are disease, ignorance, poverty, and overpopulation. Since 1936 many Egyptians had been worried about the increasing Jewish presence in Palestine. War broke out in May 1948 between Israel and all Arab countries, including Egypt. The course of the war was little short of disastrous, and laid bare the bankrupt nature of internal policies in Egypt. In July 1952 a coup d'état ousted the monarchy, and for the first time in over 2,000 years, Egypt was ruled by Egyptians.

After initial economic progress, by the mid-1960s a period of economic hardship set in. From 1967, Egypt's economic situation deteriorated rapidly, and there was a visible resurgence of religious groups. The regime did not allow the population a real share in government but did give them the semblance of participation. Because of overpopulation and the decline of agriculture, there has been progressive depopulation of the countryside and increasing urbanization.

This review of the history of modern Egypt demonstrates the central paradox of Egyptian identity—the alienation of Egyptians from their rulers. That is why Egyptians hold so strongly to their religion. Alcohol consumption is restricted in Egyptian religion and always has been. Recent Egyptian culture is also reactionary to Western culture, which has a morality that generally permits alcohol consumption.

The Campaign Against Distilled Spirits in Europe

Patrick Dillon

When the process of distillation, which uses heat to increase the concentration of alcohol in fermented beverages, was first intro-duced in Europe in the sixteenth century, it was seen as alchemy, or the magical transformation of ordinary wine. As Patrick Dil-lon describes in this selection, distilled spirits were called aqua vitae, the water of life, and said to have limitless medical pow-ers—spirits were good for the eyes, cured palsy and scurvy, and most important, protected against the plague. But their use, Dil-lon writes, did not diminish when those claims proved false. In-stead, spirits became cheaper and readily available, leading quickly to drunkenness and health problems. As a result, govern-ments issued edicts against alcohol as early as the fifteenth cen-tury. Patrick Dillon is a British architect whose expertise focuses on the eighteenth century. He has acted as a consultant on the redevelopment of London's Benjamin Franklin House and has written two crime novels, Truth *and* Lies.

I t started as alchemy.

It started with secrets. The Greeks knew how to take the salt out of sea water. Chemists of the Levant brewed mysteri-ous potions in odd-shaped vessels. When Henry II's soldiers raided monasteries in Ireland in the twelfth century, they sometimes came across casks of a heady liquid they didn't rec-ognise. The liquid was hot on the tongue and burned their throats. Just a few gulps could leave them roaring drunk.

When the magic of distilling began to be whispered around Europe in the late Middle Ages, it was 'Books of Secrets' [collections of chemical, alchemical, and medical recipes] which passed on the formulae. Distilling transformed the nature of matter, and that had always been the alchemist's dream. The distiller put ordinary wine into his still. He lit a fire beneath it. And at the touch of the fire's wand, a mysterious transformation took place. Vapour rose from the broad base of the still to its narrow neck, condensed, then dripped from the spout. What the distiller collected in the vessel he had waiting was clear and odd-smelling, slightly oily. It was nothing like the wine he had started with; nature had been transformed. The distiller had reached out and placed one hand on the philosopher's stone.

The philosopher's stone produced the elixir of life, and that was the name distillers gave to the clear, pungent liquid that dripped from their stills. It became aqua vitae, eau de vie, usquebaugh, the water of life. No one doubted its power. Distilled spirits were the new wonder-drugs in the apothecaries' cabinet. Their medical possibilities seemed limitless. They cured palsy and prevented scurvy, some claimed. They were good for the eyes. They would even protect drinkers from the most terrible scourge of all, the plague. An English doctor [named de Mayerne] who set down his own recipe not long before the terrible outbreak of 1665 boasted that 'this water . . . must be kept as your life, and above all earthly treasure . . . All the Plague time . . . trust to this; for there was never man, woman, or child that failed of their expectation in taking it.'

The ingredients distillers put into their stills were exotic, the recipes complex and fantastical. One, of 1559, was for 'a certain Aqua Vita such as is made at Constantinople in the Emperor's Court.' The most refined of all spirits were 'compound waters' (*aquae compositae*), which were made in two separate processes. First a raw spirit was distilled, usually from wine. Then a complex bouquet of flavourings was added to the spirit, and it was distilled again. This time, the liquid which dripped from the still carried with it a powerful aroma and taste. Its flavourings were herbs from the medieval medicine chest, spices carried halfway across the world in small sealed boxes: 'rue, sage, lavender, marjoram, wormwood, rosemary, red roses, thistle, pimpernel, valerian, juniper berries, bay berries, angelica, citrus bark, coriander, sandalwood, basil, grain of paradise, pepper, ginger, cinnamon, saffron, mace, nutmeg, cubeb, cardamon, galingall.' It was no coincidence that the flavoured spirit called gin would be developed in Holland and England, the two countries that would dominate the spice trade.

Spirits Flood Europe

Time soon showed that the alchemists had missed the philosopher's stone again. Spirits didn't grant eternal life; they didn't even cure the plague. But they did have other effects. Even the most earnest doctor couldn't help noticing that. Spirit-drinking 'sharpeneth ye wit,' one wrote. 'It maketh me merry & preserveth youth . . . It agreeth marvellously . . . with man's nature.' Spirits may not have conquered death, but they did make life more palatable. Compared to distilled spirits, beer and wine were just flavoured water.

Something else was about to become clear as well. You didn't have to be philosopher, alchemist or magician to make these powerful new drugs. You didn't even need a ready source of wine. They could be distilled from anything—even from grain, the staple food of northern Europe. Soon, on a tour to the Baltic, the Dutchman Caspar Coolhaes [a clergyman] noticed that, 'in Danzig, Königbergen and similar White Sea towns, just like in our countries at Amsterdam and neighbourhood and also at Rotterdam, Hoorn, Enkhuyzen and other towns, corn-distilleries were founded.' Lucas Bols established his distillery near Amsterdam in 1572. [The city of] Schiedam was growing as the home of the Dutch distilling industry by the 1630s. The stage was set for Europe to be flooded with a cheap and intoxicating new drug.

That was a more dangerous kind of magic, and many were scared of it. Way back in 1450, a Brandenburg Codex [law] had tried to slam shut the lid of Pandora's box. 'Nobody,' it decreed, 'shall serve aquavit or give it to his guests.' [The German city of] Augsburg legislated in 1570 against grain spirits as 'harmful to the health, and a useless waste of wheat.' In France, where distilling would remain focused on wine, rather than grain, brandy was banned in 1651. In Russia the rapid spread of vodka-drinking led to a panic clamp-down on drinking houses in 1652. Neither measure lasted long. But in 1677, only five years after the ban had been replaced by taxes, the Paris authorities again noted the spread of the *limonadiers* [sellers of drinks], and warned against 'those sorts of liqueurs of which the excess is incomparably more dangerous than that of wine.'

Quick Intoxication, Long Oblivion

That was the nub of it. Spirits weren't just stronger versions of wine or beer; they were different in kind, more destabilising, more dangerous. Beer and wine had been around for centuries. They were hallowed by tradition, ingrained in the woodwork; the tavern and alehouse reeked of them. Beer-drinkers raised their flagons in the same room where their grandfathers had drunk. When they broke into song, they didn't threaten the order of things; they were figures of fun. [Shakespeare's character] Falstaff was a cheery and familiar presence. By contrast, the new spirits were gaunt strangers in town. They took up residence in bare cellars and rooms behind shops; their devotees were vicious and unpredictable. Instead of good cheer and old drinking songs, spirits offered quick intoxication, then long oblivion.

Maybe the aura of magic never left distilling. Spirits would always reek of alchemy, of the dark arts. When English reformers came to revile spirit-drinking in the early eighteenth century, they saw gin not just as different in degree from beer, but worse, different in kind. 'Man,' wrote the [anti-alcohol] campaigner Dr Stephen Hales in 1734, 'not contented with what his bountiful and munificent creator intend[ed] for his comfort . . . has unhappily found means to extract, from what God intended for his refreshment, a most pernicious and intoxicating liquor. The distiller was a second snake in the garden of Eden; gin-drinking was a second fall. Madam Geneva [gin] was not only unholy but unnatural as well, part whore and part witch.

By the time Dr Stephen Hales began his campaign, five million gallons of raw spirits were being distilled in London every year. The most common drink in the slums, flavoured with juniper berries, had once been called Geneva, after the Dutch name for juniper spirits. But by then it had 'by frequent use and the laconic spirit of the nation, from a word of middling length, shrunk into a monosyllable, intoxicating GIN.'

The Gin Craze of Eighteenth-Century England

Jessica Warner

When gin suddenly became both cheap and easy to obtain in about 1720, London's working classes quickly adopted it as the drug of choice for the roughly thirty-year period now known as the "gin craze." In this selection taken from her book Craze: Gin and Debauchery in an Age of Reason, *Jessica Warner describes the drinking culture of London during the first half of the eighteenth century. She explains that a populace accustomed to drinking beer and ale expected to be able to drink gin in the same way—by the pint—but the much higher alcohol content of gin quickly caused serious health problems. The problems impacted women and children as well as men, worsening conditions in already blighted slums. Warner also analyzes the anti-gin laws passed during that era, arguing that English lawmakers only became concerned about gin consumption when they were not occupied with foreign wars. Jessica Warner is a professor of history at the University of Toronto and a research scientist at Toronto's Centre for Addiction and Mental Health.*

Cheap, widely available, and several times stronger than the traditional alcoholic beverages of the English working classes, gin was the first modern drug. Its enormous popularity gave rise to what has since come to be known as the gin craze, which is generally viewed as having started in 1720 and ended in 1751. In 1700, the average adult drank slightly more than a third of a gallon of cheap spirits over the course of a year; by 1720 that amount had nearly doubled; and by 1729, the year when the first act restricting sales of gin was passed, the number had nearly doubled again, to slightly more than

1.3 gallons per capita. The figures include only the population fifteen years of age or older, although there were as yet no formal restrictions on minors' access to alcohol. In 1743 annual consumption peaked at 2.2 gallons per capita, after which the craze at long last started to abate. By 1752, the year after the passage of the final gin act, annual per capita consumption had fallen by nearly one half, to 1.2 gallons, only to drop by half again by 1757. From this point on annual consumption remained fairly constant for the next two decades, at about 0.6 gallons per capita.

Unlike beer and ale, which had for centuries been the traditional beverages of the poor, gin's effects were instantaneous, leaving "a Man . . . no time to recollect or think, whether he has had enough or not. The Smallness of the Quantity deceives him, so that his Reason is gone before he is aware." Time and time again men and women who might ordinarily have drunk a pint or two of beer drank a pint or two of gin instead, often with disastrous consequences. A man described as a "Plush Weaver" [a weaver of plush fabric] drank a quart of gin in less than half an hour. The following morning he drank another "Pint at a Draught [at one gulp]"; by day's end he was reportedly "raving mad." A week later a laborer by the name of George Wade went to a public house [pub] in Westminster [part of London], "drank a Pint of Gin off at a Draught, and expired in a few minutes." A group of men in Newington Green [a London park] "persuaded a poor Labourer, in a Frolick, as they call'd it, to drink three or four Pints of Gin giving him a Shilling for each Pint, which he had no sooner done, but he fell down, and died immediately." A man and his pregnant wife died in very similar circumstances, having shared nearly two bottles between them.

The dates, 1720 to 1751, are arbitrary at best. Consumption had been rising steadily before 1720, and it was actually higher in 1717 than it would be in 1720. The year 1751 is equally arbitrary. Demand had in fact peaked back in 1743, and while the Gin Act of 1751 doubtless had a salutary effect on consumption, it was not until 1757, when a succession of crop failures forced the government to ban the use of domestic grains in distilling, that consumption actually dropped below the levels reached in the early 1720s. The dates do, however, have the advantage of corresponding to how contemporaries perceived events: few people worried publicly about gin before 1720, and just as few people worried publicly about it after 1751. . . .

Concerns and Problems Did Not Coincide

In the case of the gin craze, concerns over drunkenness bore very little correspondence to actual consumption, begging the question of whether a reforming elite was reacting to gin *per se* or rather to larger and more intractable threats to their society and way of life. This is the same critical question that confronts us in our own responses to drugs and the people who use them.

In the case of gin, consumption peaked in the early 1740s, while complaints—and the laws enacted in response to them—peaked much earlier, in the 1730s. Parliament, in other words, paid attention to gin only when it actually had the time to take on issues that it might otherwise safely ignore. And so four of the eight gin acts were passed in the otherwise uneventful 1730s, compared to just two in the turbulent 1740s. These last two, moreover, were designed not to impose sobriety on the working poor, but simply to raise new funds for fighting the War of Austrian Succession (1740–1748). The real pattern behind the gin acts was very simple: people worried about gin when very little else seemed to be happening—and when the government was flush. And so people worried about gin and passed laws against it in times of peace, and conveniently forgot about it in times of war. Or, rather, they did not so much forget about gin as choose to treat it as just another source of revenue. Two centuries later, in 1933, another legislature [the U.S. Congress] would also find itself short of funds; soon after this realization, it put an end to Prohibition by passing the Twenty-first Amendment.

Analogies, however, can be a tricky business, especially when they are drawn between two very different societies. Three hundred years ago, when gin was just starting to become popular in England, there was no police force in the modern sense of the word. In principle, justices of the peace worked for free, as did the male citizens who were forced to volunteer their time as constables, in which capacity they reluctantly dragged suspects, many of whom were their friends and neighbors, before justices who were themselves often members of the same community. In most cases, moreover, the burden of prosecuting offenders fell on their victims, many of whom were naturally reluctant to spend what little time and money they had in court. The costs could be staggering. In or around 1735, for example, William Goudge spent £24—a small fortune by contemporary standards—in prosecuting three informers for perjury; this did not include the £10 that he had already paid upon wrongful conviction under the Gin Act of 1736.

Anti-Gin Reformers Wanted Stability

These are important points. For one thing, they tell us that a drug scare can occur in a society as yet lacking a police force and larger political and bureaucratic structures. The closest thing that eighteenth-century England had to a modern bureaucracy was the Excise [tax] Office, and as such its commissioners and officers were destined to play a prominent role in the war on gin. The same points also underscore the extent to which eighteenth-century England was held together not by the state and formal institutions, but rather by the willingness of most of its members to accept a status quo rife with inequalities. England was remarkable for its stability—certainly when compared to the upheavals that were to beset its more autocratic rivals on the continent—but its underlying institutions were in fact entirely fragile. The Stuarts [a British dynasty], who had been ousted back in 1658, constituted the biggest and most obvious threat to the nation's stability. In 1745 they very nearly succeeded in returning to power, reinforcing in everyone's mind just how vulnerable their kingdom and society really were. Given the essential fragility of the nation's political institutions, and given the very real external threats that existed up until 1745, it is hardly surprising that even the slightest threat to the status quo was a source of enormous alarm to the nation's governing class. Gin was one of those threats, and the men who sought to put the genie back in the bottle wanted nothing more than to return their society to a golden age that was rapidly receding into the past.

This, in turn, raises the thorny question of exactly what to call the people who fought so hard against gin and the people who drank it. They were reformers, but in what sense of the word? For one thing, their agenda was anything but egalitarian. On the contrary, they believed that their society functioned best when each member accepted his or her station in life. For most people this meant accepting a life of drudgery and poverty, leaving a lucky few with a great deal of time and money on their hands. Nobody seriously challenged this vision of society until the very end of the century, and when that challenge came, in the form of the French Revolution, England managed to survive with its institutions and social structures very much intact.

The ideological differences between the people who hated gin and those who merely tolerated it were in fact entirely subtle, and basically boiled down to this: the enemies of gin resented any form of consumerism and conspicuous consumption on the part of the poor, while the people who tolerated gin were prepared to allow the poor a certain degree of latitude in how they might spend their very limited incomes. One group looked back in time to the essentially static economic theories of the sixteenth and seventeenth centuries; the other looked forward in time to the endless possibilities promised by [philosopher] Adam Smith in *The Wealth of Nations*.

Reformers Did Not Seek Abstinence

Nor did the enemies of gin have much in common with the leaders of the great temperance movements of the nineteenth and early twentieth centuries. For one thing, they never advocated abstinence from all forms of alcohol. Nor could they have. Alcohol—be it beer, gin, wine, port, or rum—was an indispensable staple of life in eighteenth-century England, both in London and in the country. This was as true of the poor as it was of the rich, the only difference being the quality and types of alcohol that each could afford. Thomas Turner, a prosperous shopkeeper in Sussex, was a habitual drunkard, recording in his diary on numerous occasions that he "came home and went to bed drunk." [Writer] Samuel Johnson was also a notorious drunkard, being unable to drink "wine or any fermented liquor . . . because he could not do it in moderation."

Because alcohol was ubiquitous in English society and because it was a major source of both taxes and employment, no one, the enemies of gin least of all, had any intention of imposing abstinence on an unwilling nation. Nor were these same men themselves willing to set an example by voluntarily abstaining from strong drink. At most they hoped to set the clock back to the years before gin had supposedly corrupted the morals and work habits of the working poor. Their social vision could, in a moment of extreme political weakness, be imposed from above—but never accepted from below. Its glaring inconsistencies were not wasted on Caleb D'Anvers, a pseudonym used by [author] Nicholas Amhurst when he routinely attacked the Ministry [government] in [the weekly publication] *The Craftsman*. "The *common People*," he wrote in August of 1736, "are highly obliged to Those, who take so much Care of Them; but why should not some Care be taken of the *great People*, as well as the *little?* For, if we are not misinform'd here, They stand in full as much Need of it."

The enemies of gin were equally inconsistent in their treatment of beer. At the time of the craze—and indeed for the duration of the century—per capita consumption of strong beer remained both high and remarkably constant, at approximately thirty gallons a year. Even so, at no point during the gin craze did anyone implicate beer in their attacks on drunkenness and its associated vices. On the contrary, even the most ardent enemies of gin encouraged workers to drink beer, believing that it would enable them to work all the harder. Even the economist Josiah Tucker, who in his heart of hearts wanted to ban the manufacture of distilled spirits altogether, recommended beer and ale on the assumption that "when laboring People use these Liquors in a *moderate* Degree, they are enabled and supported to Work the better. . . ." It also helped that the industry was well represented in Parliament, with no fewer than ten brewers being elected to the House of Commons between 1720 and 1751.

The idea that distilled spirits should be banned outright started to gain in popularity only in the early 1750s, and even then only among a handful of reformers. Two anonymous letters, one published in *The London Magazine* in March of 1751, the other in *The Gentleman's Magazine* in April of the same year, went so far as to argue that the entire industry should be suppressed. And Josiah Tucker confessed that he would favor abolishing the manufacture of all spirits in England if doing so "would put a stop to the manufacture of those liquors in all Countries." But again, these were the views of a very small minority, and it was not until the early nineteenth century, with the advent of the temperance movement, that it became fashionable to talk about banning distilled spirits altogether. It was an even greater leap to talk about banning all alcoholic beverages and not just spirits, and this did not occur until well into the nineteenth century.

Alcohol in Charles Dickens's Time

Edward Hewett and W.F. Axton

In the following selection Edward Hewett and W.F. Axton describe the love that novelist Charles Dickens had for the congenial eating and drinking customs of London before the Industrial Revolution. The authors write that Dickens knew the end had come for the era he was so fond of, with its warm inns and taverns, where alcohol flowed freely, and he tried to recreate this disappearing time in his stories. In the course of his forty-year writing career, Dickens portrayed most of his more than two thousand characters enjoying food and drink. Yet, the authors explain, he understood the reasons behind the temperance movement of the nineteenth century, given the social problems caused by the heavy drinking habits of Londoners. Edward Hewett, a writer and painter, taught art at Ohio State University and has taught painting at universities in England and the United States. W.F. Axton taught English at the University of Louisville.

Charles Dickens' artistic life began and ended in celebrating the pleasures of the flowing bowl and the groaning board. His first published sketch in 1832, "A Dinner at Poplar Walk," opens on a comfortable bachelor's breakfast, pauses over an evening brandy-and-soda, and reaches its comic catastrophe at a dinner party. The last scene that Dickens wrote before his sudden death in 1870 at the age of 58 recounts the preparations for breakfast of another bachelor, Dick Datchery. What he might have eaten is, alas! locked in the eternal silence of his creator's death; but the last word Dickens put to paper was "appetite." In between Mr. Minns [of "Poplar Walk"] and Dick Datchery, Dickens' abundant imagination breathed life

Edward Hewett and W.F. Axton, *Convivial Dickens: The Drinks of Dickens and His Times*. Athens: Ohio University Press, 1983. Reproduced by permission of Edward Hewett and the literary estate of W.F. Axton.

into well over two thousand characters during an active writing career of nearly forty years, most of whom are depicted enjoying the table and tankard.

When the novelist was a boy, gentlemen in gaiters still sat over their Rum Punch and churchwardens in the cosy, warm taprooms of coaching inns, where Old England lingered as though it would never pass away. By the end of the novelist's life a half-century later, the old inns and their sociable inhabitants were gone, together with the colorful coaches that had served them, swept away by the coming of the railroads and other profound causes of change in the fabric of English life. In their place arose those recent French importations, the restaurant and the metropolitan hotel (the latter often a hollow, drafty affair fronting a rail terminus), and that creature of native English origin on every slum corner, the gin-palace, with all its tawdry splendors of flaring gas lamps, plate glass, and stucco neo-classicism.

But Dickens perceived that, despite the wealth, power, and sheer magnitude of the new industrial world rising around him, some invaluable ingredient of the English spirit had been lost along the way, an ingredient that had been essentially tied to the robust days of careening coaches, key-bugles, galloping teams, and inviting country inns and city taverns. The "new" men, like [Dickens characters] Podsnap, Veneering, the Tite Barnacles, and their ilk, who came bobbing in the wake of industrialism and empire, led cramped, mean lives, in which the pleasures of eating and drinking were joylessly yoked to the wheel of ostentatious display. In reaction to the contrary pull of these impressions, Dickens spent his life as a writer alternately trying to re-create imaginatively that sense of humane sociability and solidarity which had marked the lost days of his youth, and satirizing the absence of these qualities in the England of his adulthood. In between these concerns, however, he always kept a sympathetically amused eye on those little social rituals of food and drink which give meaning and value to the lives of ordinary people.

The Old Coaching Days Were Over

Dickens was well aware of the fact that every activity of the daily life of Victorian England was tinctured by the social implications of eating and drinking. But Dickens' first loyalties lay with the ebullient world of the old coaching days, which he had known as a boy and which he knew was passing away even as he was writing his earliest works: the lusty, liquid setting of the open road, coaches and post-chaises, affectionate domestic kitchens and parlors, and steamily convivial country inns and city taverns.

Indeed, in *Barnaby Rudge* (1841), The Maypole Inn, [in] Chigwell, becomes an epitome of all that was best in Georgian England, all that was sociable, sane, and enduring, as opposed to the irrational, violent, and anti-social that was touched into bloody life by the anti-papist Gordon riots of 1780. Threatened by this "shameful tumult" without, the Maypole stands for England itself.

> ... All bars are snug places, but the Maypole's was the very snuggest, cosiest, and completest bar, that ever the wit of man devised. Such amazing bottles in old oaken pigeon-holes; such gleaming tankards dangling from pegs at about the same inclination as thirsty men would hold them to their lips; such sturdy little Dutch kegs ranged in rows on shelves; so many lemons hanging in separate nets ... with goodly loaves of snowy sugar stowed away hard by, of punch, idealised beyond all mortal knowledge; such closets, such presses, such drawers full of pipes, such places for putting things away in hollow window-seats, all crammed to the throat with eatables, drinkables, or savoury condiments; lastly, and to crown all ... such a stupendous cheese! ...

But the Maypole was the past, and was soon to pass away forever before a mob of rioters, in an act prophetic of the slow demise of the old, stable order, and the traditional, fraternal way of life it embodied, under the rising tide of industrialism. Liberty and equality, it turns out, negate fraternity.

But then, all things relating to flagon and trencher were rapidly changing during Dickens' lifetime. Licensing laws for ale-houses were eased after 1830, so that by the time of the novelist's first big hit, the *Pickwick Papers*, in 1836, there were nearly 50,000 new ones in the kingdom, and they totalled roughly one for every neighborhood. The modern form of the pub was also evolving during the same period into its definitive three-part configuration of public bar, tap-room, and parlor or lounge. Ever emulous of the lavish new gin-palaces, the public house developed its gaudy-dowdy but comfortable blend of polished mahogany, brass, casks and bottles, red curtains, and florid glass everywhere—bevelled, mirrored, frosted, etched, and gilded with brand names—the whole dominated by a stately parade of beer-pulls. Closer to the novelist's heart, however, was the dwindling number of independent publicans [pubkeepers] and innkeepers, like Benjamin Britain of The Nutmeg Grater Inn [from *The Battle of Life*, 1846] and the immortal if obtuse John Willet of the Maypole [from *Barnaby Rudge*, 1841], tens of thousands of whom once brewed their own ales and beers and presided over their own cheery hearths. The establishment of "off-license" premises (the beverages bought there had to be consumed elsewhere) and the national distribution of bottled ale allowed genteel folk to drink in the privacy of their homes, thereby further diminishing the free-and-easy camaraderie of inns and taverns, where travellers of every class had met and mingled. Even American cocktails, cobblers, and mint juleps were coming into fashion among the *beau monde* [fashionable world], while that cold and brittle sparkling wine, Champagne, could be found in the glass of every new-rich *arriviste* [new arrival into a social class].

Cocktails and Temperance

Inventive to a fault, the Victorians gave us both the Martini Cocktail and Temperance. While Dickens had little patience with Teetotal fanatics like his quondam [sometime] friend and illustrator, George Cruikshank, a reformed drunk, and even less with militant Sabbatarians, who wished to prohibit every form of public entertainment on the workingman's only day off in the week [the sabbath], he knew that the Temperance movement had a point. The corner local or gin-palace was virtually the only social institution available to the urban proletarian until much later in the century. That being the case, it is not surprising that at mid-century the average Englishman spent more on drink than on rent. Per-capita consumption of malt beverages averaged more than 43 imperial gallons, that of home-distilled (i.e., English-made) spirits about a gallon, and of wine (most of it the heavily fortified Iberian kind) more than half a gallon. And these figures do not include the most popular spirits of the time, brandy and rum, which were largely distilled abroad, homemade beers and wines, and smuggled and boot-legged goods, all of which taken together amounted to a considerable additional part of actual consumption. No wonder there were so many "benchers," "brewer's horses," and "loose fish"—drunkards, in short.

While Dickens lamented the passing of tavern, inn, and coach, he was no less the man who introduced the great city of London into the novel as perhaps his ultimate subject and theme. For the teeming metropolis fascinated him as it did so many writers of the time. The following is a description of early-morning London:

> The gaslit public-houses are the first shops to open in the darkness well before dawn, especially in those teeming market areas, Covent Garden and Smithfield. In the latter, the din of whistling, barking, bellowing, bleating, grunting, squeaking, and the cries of hawkers, the shouts, oaths and quarreling on all sides; the ringing of bells and roar of voices, that issue from every public house; the crowding, pushing, driving, beating, whooping, and yelling . . . quite confound the senses. From Southwark the great brewers' drays begin to rumble over the bridges; the quayside wharves and warehouses are awake, where the kegs and barrels and

hogsheads [casks] wait, of gin and rum and wine. The essential London, that feeds and gives drink to the whole, wakes and works long before the rest, getting ready for another day. And throughout the day to come till dawn breaks again, the sounds of people ordering meals, and being served them, and eating and drinking and being washed up after, are no small part of the great hum.

This "essential London" was never far from Dickens' mind and imagination. Food and drink were to him important indices to the human qualities of individuals and to the moral texture of times and places and institutions. He knew all about the private and public lives of the host of clerks, shopkeepers, merchants, and their assistants that formed the "tide of humanity" which made its way on foot into the City every morning of the week but one from its quarters in London's inner suburbs, and made its way home every evening. Along the way, as he knew, the great arterial roads and streets were lined with taverns and pubs to minister to their thirst and hunger—as many as 46 in the three-quarters of a mile of the Strand between Trafalgar Square and St. Clement's, and 49 in a mile of Whitechapel Road. So deeply embedded in the English mind was the association of travel, drink, and tavern that the first London railway termini were given such [publike] names as The Bricklayer's Arms, The Dartmouth Arms, and The Jolly Sailor; and it was some years before more descriptive names were substituted. The old coaching days and ways, it appears, were hard to kill off.

Trading Alcohol for Votes in Colonial Times

Eric Burns

Despite his charisma, George Washington lost dramatically in his first attempt to run for public office in 1755. In this selection Eric Burns describes that loss and Washington's comeback in his subsequent campaign to win a seat in the Virginia Assembly. Washington had 144 gallons of alcoholic beverages delivered to the town that had voted against him in the previous election. Burns explains that it was common for candidates to ply voters generously with strong drink and that those office seekers who objected to the practice usually lost at the polls by large margins. As Burns notes, it was important for candidates to supply large quantities of alcohol as well as demonstrate their congeniality and egalitarianism by drinking along with the voters. After Washington finished his service in office, he retired to his Mount Vernon estate and established a brewery.

Eric Burns, host of the TV program Fox News Watch, *has also written* Broadcast Blues *and* The Joy of Books.

In his early twenties, [George Washington] was an even more imposing figure than he came to be in later years, although the later years were when the painters and sculptors caught up to him, insisting that he pose for them and thereby make his immortality visible. He was "straight as an Indian," said his friend George Mercer, "measuring six feet two inches in his stockings and weighing 175 pounds. . . . In conversation he looks you full in the face, is deliberate, deferential, and engaging. His demeanor is at all times composed and dignified. His movements and features are graceful, his walk majestic, and he is a speeding horseman."

Eric Burns, *The Spirits of America: A Social History of Alcohol.* Philadelphia: Temple University Press, 2004. © by Temple University Press. All rights reserved. Used by permission of Temple University Press.

He was, in other words, a charismatic man in a critical time, an ideal candidate for public office.

Washington made his first attempt at such a position in 1755, at the age of twenty-three, seeking a seat in the Virginia Assembly. Although he would never express such a sentiment publicly, he believed that, despite his youth, he was the best man for the job in terms of both ability and attitude. The voters, however, did not; they rejected Washington overwhelmingly. There were several reasons for the defeat, but none more important than the fact that, a year or so earlier, the aspiring legislator had insulted the very people he hoped would elect him.

The French and Indian War was raging at the time, the two title groups allied against British territorial interests in the New World, hoping at the least to stop further expansion, at most to reclaim lands that the colonists had already usurped and settled. Washington distinguished himself quickly, forcing a French evacuation of Fort Duquesne, within the boundaries of today's city of Pittsburgh, and leading his men with a daring and grasp of strategy far beyond what could be expected from one with such limited military experience. Word of his triumph spread quickly; all who knew the young soldier assumed a bright future.

An Insulting Monologue

Shortly afterward, there was a lull in the fighting and Washington returned to his home colony of Virginia, hoping to rest, tend to his farm, and renew some friendships. It was not to be. Through one of those friends he learned that the nearby county of Frederick was about to be attacked by small, guerrilla-like bands of Native Americans. Some of them were already on the march, and were expected to join forces with others in a day or so, pooling their weapons and their wills. They would attack, Washington's friend told him, in less than a week.

The young soldier made his way to the county's largest town, Winchester, and not only warned the residents of the danger but urged them to resist it, to take up arms and hold their ground. He even offered to lead the local militia into battle himself, despite the fact that the jurisdiction was not his. He spoke to the men as inspirationally as he could, talking of duty and courage and responsibility to future generations.

Winchester wanted none of it. The militia colonel told Washington that his men had already heard rumors of the impending assault, and had decided on flight, not fight. Only if the natives cut off their routes of escape would they put up resistance, and most of them assumed it would not be enough, that the aggressors would overpower them and they would die with their families. It was not what they wanted, they said to their colonel, but if it was what fate had in store, so be it.

Washington was incensed. What kind of soldiers *were* these? He berated them for their pessimism, their cowardice, their unwillingness to act in their own behalf; it was a monologue of uncharacteristic severity and passion. Biographer James Thomas Flexner tells what happened next:

> Washington then went to a stable and tried to impress [compel to military service] a horse. The owner barred his way. He drew his sword and took the horse. Immediately, he was surrounded by a mob of inhabitants who, wishing to keep their animals for their own personal escapes, offered to "blow out my brains."

Washington managed to "stare them down," however, and rode out of Winchester as fast as he could, cursing the mob of inhabitants for their lack of fortitude.

Winchester's Revenge

But when the next election came along, the mob found itself with an unexpected chance to get even, for there on the ballot, next to the names of people that Winchesterites either admired or tolerated, was a single name they had lately come to revile: George Washington. For abusing them verbally, they avenged themselves electorally. Hugh West won the assembly seat that year with 271 votes. Thomas Swearingen came in second with 270. Washington finished a distant and discredited fourth with 40, which perhaps comprised the total number of Frederick Countians unfamiliar with the details of the Winchester incident. Washington was bitterly disappointed; he had not realized how deeply the feelings against him were running. He was also determined not to fail the next time.

Two years later, and two years wiser, Washington stood again for the Virginia Assembly, relying on the passage of time and the growth of his reputation to have eased hard feelings, and on rum, punch, cider, wine, and beer to have persuaded those who still *did* resent him to let bygones be bygones. Washington saw to it that 144 gallons of these beverages, in all their glorious potency, were delivered to as many polling places as possible, and he further made sure that supporters of his were stationed alongside the beverages to invite voters to indulge before making up their minds about the candidates.

Dip your mug, friend, one would say.

Colonel Washington does not want you to make so important a decision while suffering the pangs of thirst, another would chime in.

Yet another would urge that the mug be drained to the last drop, thirst being a malady known to return within seconds of what seemed a cure.

The voters drank. Still, the colonel was concerned, edgy. To the man who served as what we would today call his campaign manager, Washington had previously expressed the hope that he had not spent with too sparing a hand.

Booze Buys Votes

He had not. The eventual father of his country got 68 more votes than runner-up Thomas Bryan Martin. West, seeking reelection, found himself 100 votes in arrears of the winner and Swearingen 350 behind. W. J. Rorabaugh analyzes the results of Washington's strategy as follows: "For his 144 gallons of refreshment, he received 307 votes, a return on his investment of better than two votes per gallon."

Washington did not originate the practice of trading booze for votes. It was a common one at the time, and was known to many, more colorfully than clearly, as "swilling the planters with bumbo." More often than not, the office-seeker joined the planters in swilling, the man and his constituents loading up their glasses and then tipping them back like friends of long standing, toasting the former's success at the latter's hands, and as soon as the glasses were empty refilling them and toasting again.

But it was not just the quantity of alcohol made available by a candidate that mattered at the time; no less important to the outcome of an election was his "manner and style of dispensing it." Rorabaugh writes of a contest a few years later than Washington's and many miles to the south. "The favored aspirant in one Mississippi election," he relates, "poured drinks for the voters with so much personal attention that it seemed like he would win. After his liquor was gone, his opponent, a Methodist minister, announced to the crowd that he also had whiskey to dispense, but that he would not be so stingy as to measure it out. 'Come forward, one and all,' he invited, 'and help yourselves.' The generous person won."

The Higher the Proof the Greater the Turnout

In addition to revealing generosity, a candidate supplied liquor to those at the polls, and drank a fair measure of the product himself in their presence, to demonstrate his "good nature and congeniality in his cups . . . thereby confirm[ing] his egalitarianism." In other words, he showed that he was a leader by providing the spirits and that he was one of the boys by quaffing them openly and sociably. In a fledgling republic, it was an unbeatable combination.

Not to mention a much-appreciated show of gratitude. There was a feeling at the time "that voters deserved recompense when so many traveled so far to exercise the suffrage." The higher the proof, the greater the recompense. And the larger the turnout; as historian Arthur M. Schlesinger has written, the presence of alcohol at the colonial polling place had "the beneficial effect" of drawing large crowds to democracy.

Still, not everyone approved. As early as 1705, a Virginia statute forbade this kind of electioneering. In 1753, an editorial in the *New York Independent Reflector* "expressed dismay that so many persons should barter their franchise for 'Beer and Brandy.'" And in 1791, a Frenchman named Ferdinard Bayard was journeying through Virginia, keeping a sharp eye on the customs of the new nation and reporting back to his friends at home, who were in the midst of a revolution of their own. He took in the doings at the polls with dismay. He saw "the candidates offer drunkenness openly to anyone who is willing to give them his vote." He saw the voters accept the offers, the buying and selling of democracy, and for so ignoble a medium of exchange. He did not know that the United States, so admirable by most contemporary accounts, had so unsavory a side.

Had M. Bayard gotten to North Carolina in his travels, he might have been even more appalled. It was reported that, on one election day in the colony, a man seeking office drove up to his local courthouse in a wagon "with a couple of tin cups, and a ten-gallon keg between his legs." He jumped to the ground, secured his horse, and began energetically emptying the keg into the cups, circulating the cups among the voters until the keg was empty and he had won their virtually unanimous support at the polls. That it was registered with foggy eyes and shaky hands, and that some of the registrants did not remember their support the next morning, probably did not trouble the new electee.

The Corrupting Influence of "Spirituous Liquors"

And a few decades later, a fellow named George D. Prentice was asked to report on the polls in another southern state for a publication called the *New England Weekly Review*. It was an assignment he never forgot. "An election in Kentucky lasts three days," Prentice wrote, never having been exposed to such a marathon before, "and during that period whiskey and apple toddy flow through our cities and villages like the Euphrates through ancient Babylon."

The most prominent foe of campaigning by whiskey and toddy in early America was James Madison, who, running for reelection to the Virginia Assembly in 1777, decided to take the high road: he would not debase the electoral process by bribing the voters with alcohol, would not create a carnival atmosphere at a serious venue. He explained that "the corrupting influence of spirituous liquors, and other treats" was "inconsistent with the purity of moral and republican virtues." It was an admirable position, a principled stand; Madison's reward was a smashing defeat at the polls, his first and only. Like Washington, he found a brilliant career in politics delayed by insufficient regard for constituent thirst.

Others objected to booze at the polls because it deemphasized the content of a candidate's character and granted him office for the content of his casks. "I guess Mr. A. is the fittest man of the two," opined a woman of the time in South Carolina, analyzing the results of a local race, "but t' other whiskies the best." It was the latter for whom the woman voted.

With the passage of time, the use of alcoholic beverages to purchase elective office became less and less common. Existing laws against it came to be enforced; new laws were passed and taken seriously by authorities; dignity and positions on issues began to count more than persuasion by potables. Yet the tradition persisted in a few races and in a few places, not only through colonial times but into the nineteenth century and even, in one comical instance, up to the dawn of the twentieth. In his book *The Big Spenders*, journalist and bon vivant Lucius Beebe tells of a man who went pointlessly, and expensively, overboard. It was "Montana's peerless Senator William Andrew Clark who, when seeking election to the United States Senate at the turn of the [twentieth] century, miscalculated by a comma the population of the city of Butte, Montana, and provided the free distribution among 45,000 enfranchised voters sufficient whisky for 450,000."

George Washington's Brewery

After his years as president, years when an estimated one out of every four dollars that Americans spent on household expenses went toward the purchase of alcohol, George Washington retired to Mount Vernon, settling into a routine to which he had aspired ever since his hiatus during the French and Indian War. He rose with the sun, ate and drank breakfast, and rode across some of his 8,000 acres to inspect both crops and men, diligent about it, [Roman general and statesman] Cincinnatus in his natural habitat. Either before or immediately after the ride, he spoke with his gardener, asking him how the shrubs were doing, what flowers should be planted next and when, whether patches of the lawn needed to be fertilized or sections of the fence mended. The gardener was a man whom Washington respected greatly, and whom he compensated not only in cash, but with "a generous allotment of rum," if not the expensive Barbados variety.

Later, perhaps after a nap, Washington took a walk, retracing some of his morning paths. Most days, he followed the walk with a cup of tea. Upon finishing, he might receive visitors; he did so almost daily, and when night fell, he wrote letters by candlelight, keeping up as best he could with the voluminous mail he received himself.

He also made his own liquor, not only for personal consumption but for sale, a decision he owed at least in part to his estate manager, James Anderson, "who persuaded Washington to turn over one of his unprofitable small farms to raising rye for whiskey. Soon Washington had a thriving operation that turned a profit of £83 in 1798, producing not only whiskey but apple, peach and persimmon brandy."

In addition, Washington built a brewery on the grounds to produce a molasses-based beer, which he savored both in the tasting and the sharing with guests. They would drink it at meals, and sometimes unaccompanied by food, as they sat in large chairs on the veranda, looking out on the Potomac and across to the federal city, still under construction but already bearing the name of Mount Vernon's master.

The Early
Temperance Crusade

Eliza Daniel Stewart

In 1872 temperance activist Eliza Daniel Stewart delivered a lecture in which she asked women to support Ohio's Adair law, giving wives or mothers of men who abused alcohol the right to sue sellers of liquor. In this firsthand account "Mother Stewart," as she referred to herself, recalls how that lecture led to her appearance in court on behalf of Mary Hukins, a woman suing the saloon where her husband drank. Despite the rage of the defense attorney, who argued that no woman had the right to address the court, the jury decided in favor of Hukins. Mother Stewart first gained leadership experience working in the Sanitary Commission, which later became the Red Cross. She later took a prominent role in the founding of the Ohio Women's Christian Temperance Union. Her 1876 speaking tour in England led to the formation of the British Women's Temperance Union.

I prepared a lecture which I delivered on January 22, 1872, in Allen's Hall [in Cincinnati, Ohio], to a large and intelligent audience. As far as I know, this was the first lecture on the subject of temperance delivered by a lady in our city. Here I date my first important movement in my temperance warfare, though I had, as opportunity offered, lectured elsewhere on the subject. It may, indeed, because of results that grew out of it, be called my first step in the [Ohio Women's] Crusade [against alcohol]. And I find it necessary, in the interest of historic truth, to give a large share of credit to my warm friend and advisor in all the years of my labors and trials, C. M. Nichols, Editor of the *Springfield Republic*, as the originator of the Crusade.... Mr. Nichols was at the meeting and-from an extended report in the *Republic* of the next day, January 23d, I copy the following:

Eliza Daniel Stewart, *Memories of the Crusade: A Thrilling Account of the Great Uprising of the Women of Ohio in 1873, Against the Liquor Crime.* Columbus, OH: Hubbard, 1888.

"The Liquor Traffic, How to Fight It. Mrs. E. D. Stewart's address at Allen's Hall, on Monday evening, Jan. 22nd. The Law and the Gospel. Allen's Hall was well filled Monday evening on the occasion of an address on the Liquor Traffic by Mrs. E. D. Stewart. The speaker gave an expression of her feeling of unfitness for so important a task as that assigned her, and then proceeded in an interesting and able address to show that she was fitted in an eminent degree for the performance of just such a work." . . .

At the close of my address, Mr. Nichols came to me and suggested that I ask the ladies of the audience to pledge themselves to hunt up the drunkards' wives and encourage them to prosecute the rum-sellers under the [Ohio] Adair law [giving wives or mothers of drunk men the right to sue the supplier of liquor], for selling to their husbands, and to stand by them in doing so. The ladies readily responded by a rising vote. But, while I knew that they then meant it, I felt quite sure that most of them would falter if a test should come. It was years ago, and before the Crusade and custom had made it comparatively easy to do such work.

Those ladies would today cheerfully pledge themselves, and keep their pledge too. A wonderful growth has occurred through the education and courage received in the Crusade, as well as the spiritual baptism that came down upon the women.

Attending Court

Two days after our meeting, I called at the *Republic* office, when Mr. Nichols exclaimed: "Oh, see here! a case under the Adair law is being tried right now in Justice Miller's court. Get some of your ladies and go in." I had my misgivings about getting the ladies, but did not say so. I knew better than a gentleman could, what the effect upon woman's mind had been of the all-time teaching that they must not seem to know anything about the saloon or men's drinking, it was not lady-like.

I went at once and called on one lady, but she was "busy and could not go." So I went in alone and sat till the court adjourned for dinner. I could not help noticing that the good old justice, who was a Christian man, was gratified at my presence, as was also the prosecuting attorney, my young friend, G.C. Rawlins, and of course the defense was not.

When the court adjourned, I hastened off to the eastern part of the city, where I felt quite sure I should find some ladies upon whom I could rely. But "they all, with one exception, began to make excuses." The exception was Mrs. S.M. Foos, a lady whose heart always goes out to the sorrowing, the needy, and the friendless. Where a friend is needed, there is she, walking in the footsteps of the lowly one. And though wealth, brilliant talents, social position, all give her open sesame [access] into the most fashionable circles, she chooses to walk in the path the Master [Jesus] hath trod, giving her life to good works and alms deeds. Yes, she would come as soon as she could dispose of some home duties.

The Testimony Begins

Upon my return to the court room, the attorney for the prosecution asked me if I would not make the opening plea to the jury. I answered that I could not think of such a thing. He insisted that I could do it. I protested that the thing was impossible. But he, intent upon winning his case, this being the first and a test case under the Adair law in our city, was disposed to avail himself of all the means he could bring to bear, and still urged me to it. I began to think right fast, and asked if he thought I could do any good by it, adding that I came in to give encouragement to the court, himself and that poor woman. "Yes," he responded, "I know you can." Then, I said, I will think of it. "Very well," he replied, "if you decide to do it, let me know, and I will show you the law to read to the jury." Taking my paper and pencil, I took notes of the testimony as the case proceeded. And I do know the Lord helped me, for new as was the work, and strange and novel my situation and surroundings, and weak the testimony, I was enabled to catch the strongest points in clear and concise form. No one, I am sure, could be more surprised at this than myself. The testimony being mainly from the habitués of the saloons, was weak and unreliable. Some of them deliberately and without flinching perjured themselves. One for the prosecution, the justice ordered from the stand.

The strongest witness, with one exception, was the little son of the drunkard, a child some ten years old, having been permitted by the justice to be sworn, because of his intelligence and manly bearing, though legally under age. The court room was crowded with saloon-keepers and their customers, a motley crowd, blear-eyed, bloated, bruised, dirty, unsightly, degraded humanity. The attorney for the defense was one of the ablest lawyers of the bar, always the liquor men's advocate. There sat that pitiful, friendless woman and her two little boys, in their scant and faded garments, alone. The wretched husband and father had by some means been spirited away out of reach.

Toward evening I went to Mr. Rawlins and asked him how near the testimony was in. "It is almost in," said he; "will you address the jury?" I said I would try. He then handed me the book, pointing out the portion to be read to the jury. I took it and familiarized myself with it. By this time the testimony being closed, Mr. Rawlins addressed the court, saying he wished to make a few remarks and also a request. The request was that Mrs. Stewart be permitted to make the opening plea to the jury.

Addressing the Jury

Of course the court had no right to object, as I, or any one else may, in our State, appear in a case before a Justice's or Mayor's court. But none but admitted lawyers may appear before the upper courts. Besides, I saw that the Justice was very willing that I should, and the opposite counsel had to acquiesce, though I saw by the ill-concealed smile, while he mumbled something that I could not quite catch, that he was saying to himself, "Now we will have fun. This old woman will make a muddle of it, and a fool of herself, and we will have rare fun picking her to pieces."

I took my law book in hand, and addressing the jury, said I found myself in a novel position, but I made this attempt to plead the case of my sister, because I knew I could speak for her as no man could. I then read the law, adding, they needed no comment on it from me. They understood its meaning. I was glad that now our women might come into the courts and prosecute the rum-seller for the destruction of their husbands and homes. I was glad, too, that in my State were men, good and true, before whom these cases might be tried. (I may say here, that while this was the nicest sugar-plum I had, it was well deserved in this case, for they were all good and true men.) I then took up the points of testimony I had caught and showed that the man, when not under the influence of liquor, was a kind husband and father, providing for the necessities of his family. That even when occasionally giving way to his appetite it had been proven that he was able to earn from $6 to $9 per week. But through the influence of drink furnished by the man now arraigned, he had become so worthless and incompetent that the wife and mother, besides her regular domestic duties, was obliged to labor to earn the means of support for her family. Yes, it was said the drunkard's wife may come into court and prosecute for the ruin of her husband, but who will stand by her? Who will befriend her? Who will defend her? And you see the array against her. I simply waved my hand towards that motley mass without looking towards them, but saw that the jury did. I proceeded to say, this woman, who I hoped would pardon me, was branded as the drunkard's wife, and must wear the brand forever. And you noticed that as on the witness stand, being strung up to the utmost tension, she detailed her sufferings and wrongs—a sight to touch and melt the stoutest heart to pity—that crowd stood there leering and jeering in satanic mirth at her misery. And these little boys, as they had noticed, precocious and intelligent beyond their years, were branded, and would carry the brand to the grave—*The Drunkard's Child*.

In closing I charged the jury that they deal with this woman as they would that others should deal with their wife or daughter. And as they dealt with her, might God deal with them. I had not spoken five minutes till I saw that I held the jury in my hand, but did not know the extent of the mischief I had done the dealer in woe till his attorney arose to defend him. If he had prepared any defense for his client, he certainly had forgotten it. He gesticulated vehemently, declared it was "infamous to bring a female in to influence the court and jury. He should think Mrs. Stewart would be ashamed to thus come into court. She had much better have been at home attending to her legitimate duties."

The Verdict

The jury, after a brief retirement, brought in a verdict of $100 and costs. This, as I have said, was the first case that had come up under the Adair law in our courts, and considering the desperate fight made by the defense, aided by his associates in the business, and the weakness of the testimony for reasons already stated, it was decided to be a very fair verdict. Of course the liquor vender appealed to the upper courts, where the "female" was not permitted by the law of the State to go into the courts to influence jury, or anyone else. But, after long delay, and staving off, and the liquor men boasting that they had money enough to fight that poor, friendless woman as long as she chose—the lower court was sustained, except the damage was cut down to $40, if I remember correctly.

The unheard-of occurrence of a woman pleading a case in court, produced quite a sensation. The papers sent it abroad, far and near, and the lawyers and other gentlemen of the city so chaffed my good friend, Esq. Spence, for letting an old lady beat him, that he became quite unfriendly towards me. And I, having noticed that while he was speaking to some point of law as the case progressed, the foreman laid his head back and slept, could not resist the temptation to tell him that I could keep the jury awake and he could not. I am most happy to record here, however, that Mr. Spence, who is my near neighbor, is to-day one of the very warmest friends I have, though we differ widely on the temperance question, I am sorry to say. The *Springfield Advertiser* of the next day gives the following report of the case:

Argument of Mrs. E. D. Stewart to a Jury in the Whisky Case—Mother Stewart in the Role of a Lawyer.

Geo. C. Rawlins, Esq., brought suit against Barnet Trickler for Mrs. Mary Hukins before Esquire Miller, laying damages at $300 for the sale of liquor to her husband. Mrs. Stewart was present and heard the evidence in the case. When it was all submitted and the case was closed as far as the evidence was concerned, Mr. Rawlins addressed the court, stating that Mrs. Stewart had been present, and heard all the evidence, and he requested that she be granted permission to address the jury on behalf of the plaintiff. The court granted the request, and Mrs. Stewart, taking a ponderous volume in her hand, proceeded to address the jury. The argument she made on this occasion was one worthy of her sex and of the bar. She was placed in such a position that she could appreciate the situation. It was a woman speaking in behalf of one of her sex, and she could portray to the jury the circumstances of the injustice, cruelty and hardships which Mrs. Hukins suffered from the whisky-seller. Mrs. Stewart spoke for a half an hour, and alluded with telling effect to the sneers which had greeted the poor woman, Mrs. Hukins, when on the stand. She also spoke of the moneyed interest which backed up the defense.

George Spence, Esq., followed Mrs. Stewart, and attributed to women all the rights which they claimed, but stated that this manifestation was for the purpose of working upon the prejudices of the jury.

Mrs. Rawlins closed the argument in the case and paid a high compliment to the speech of Mrs. Stewart. The jury returned a verdict of $100 for the plaintiff.

THE HISTORY
OF DRUGS

CHAPTER 2

Alcohol Use in the Twentieth Century

Society's Changing Attitude Toward Alcohol

David F. Musto

*In this selection David F. Musto describes the way Americans'
view of alcohol use has changed from the founding of the country through the 1990s. Until well into the nineteenth century,
most Americans drank very heavily, believing that strong alcoholic drinks provided major health benefits. Usage decreased
with the rise of the temperance movement, which at first pro-
moted moderation only. Abstinence became a goal well after the
movement began. By 1855 about one-third of all Americans
lived under prohibition laws. Those laws fell into disuse during
the Civil War era, when the government needed revenue from
the liquor tax. The Women's Crusade against saloons revitalized
the anti-alcohol movement in the 1870s, and in 1920 the Eighteenth Amendment for national prohibition was passed. However, the law, Musto explains, was "a blatant failure" and did
not stop the majority of Americans from drinking. After its repeal in 1933, alcohol usage surged again, following roughly 70–
year cycles of disapproval and tolerance. Musto describes a third
era of temperance beginning in about 1980 and focusing on
drunk driving and fetal alcohol syndrome. David F. Musto, professor of child psychiatry and the history of medicine at Yale
University, served on the alcohol policy panel of the National
Academy of Sciences and is considered a leading historian of
drug policy in the United States. He has written extensively on
drug and alcohol policy issues.*

The young American ship of state floated on a sea of distilled spirits. In the period immediately after the American Revolution, a generally favorable view of alcoholic bever-

ages coincided with rising levels of consumption that far exceeded any in modern times. By the early decades of the 19th century, Americans drank roughly three times as much alcohol as they . . . [did at the end of the 20th century].

The country also had its abstemious side. Even as consumption of alcohol was reaching unprecedented levels, an awareness of the dangers of drink began to emerge, and the first American temperance movement took hold. At its peak in 1855, 13 of 40 states and territories had adopted legal prohibition. By the 1870s, public opinion had turned back, and liquor was flowing freely again; then, around the turn of the century, a movement for abstinence gained steam, culminating in the 13-year experiment of Prohibition that began in 1920.

Over the history of the U.S., popular attitudes and legal responses to the consumption of alcohol and other mood-altering substances have oscillated from toleration to a peak of disapproval and back again in cycles roughly 70 years long. Although other nations appear to have embraced the virtues of moderation, the U.S. continues to swing slowly back and forth between extremes.

Cycles of Approval and Rejection

The length of these trends may explain why most people are unaware of our repetitive history. Few contemporary Americans concerned about the abuse of illegal drugs, for example, know that opiate use was also a burning issue in the first decades of the 20th century, just as few of today's nutrition and exercise enthusiasts know about their health-minded predecessors from the same period.

Furthermore, a phenomenon analogous to political correctness seems to control discourse on alcohol and other "vices": when drinking is on the rise and most believe that liquor poses little risk to life and health, temperance advocates are derided as ignorant and puritanical; in the end stage of a temperance movement, brewers, distillers, sellers and drinkers all come under harsh attack. Citizens may come of age with little knowledge of the contrary experiences of their forebears. Even rigorous studies that contradict current wisdom may be ignored—data showing both the damaging and beneficial effects of alcohol appear equally susceptible to suppression, depending on the era.

It now appears that a third era of temperance is under way in the U.S. Alcohol consumption peaked around 1980 and has since fallen by about 15 percent. The biggest drop has been in distilled spirits, but wine use has also waned. Beer sales have fallen less, but nonalcoholic brews—replicas of Prohibition's "near beer"—have been rising in popularity.

The shift in attitude is apparent in the cyclic movement of the legal drinking age. In 1971 the 26th Amendment to the Constitution—the most rapidly ratified in the nation's history—lowered the voting age to 18. Soon after, many state legislatures lowered the drinking age to conform to the voting age. Around 1980, however, states started rolling back the drinking age to 21. Surprisingly, the action was praised even among the 18- to 20-year-olds it affected. In 1984 the U.S. government, which cannot itself mandate a national drinking age, threatened to withhold federal highway funds from any state or territory that did not raise its drinking age to 21. Within a short time every state and the District of Columbia were in compliance. Puerto Rico has been the only holdout.

Alcohol, Driving, and Youth

Drunk driving is the most recent catalyst for public activism against alcohol abuse. At the end of the 1970s, two groups appeared with the goal of combating alcohol-related accidents: Remove Intoxicated Drivers (RID) on the East Coast and Mothers Against Drunk Driving (MADD) in California. Both groups attacked weak drunk-driving laws and judicial laxness, especially in cases where drivers may have been repeatedly arrested for drunk driving—including some who had killed others in crashes—but never imprisoned.

Across the nation RID and MADD have strengthened the drunk-driving laws. Although sometimes at odds with each other, both have successfully lobbied for laws reducing the legal threshold of intoxication, increasing the likelihood of incarceration and suspending drivers' licenses without a hearing if their blood alcohol levels exceed a state's legal limit, typically about 0.1 percent.

In 1981 Students Against Driving Drunk (SADD) was established to improve the safety of high school students. The group promotes a contract between parents and their children in which the children agree to call for transportation if they have been drinking, and the parents agree to provide it. As a result, however, RID and MADD have accused SADD of sanctioning youthful drinking rather than trying to eliminate it.

The Campaign Against Alcohol Use

Political action has reinforced the prevailing public beliefs. In 1988 Congress set up the Office of Substance Abuse Prevention (OSAP) under the auspices of the Department of Health and Human Services. The OSAP provided what it called "editorial guidelines" to encourage media to adopt new ways of describing drug and alcohol use. Instead of referring to "responsible use" of alcohol, for example, the office suggested that newspapers and magazines should speak simply of "use, since there is a risk associated with all use." This language suggests that there is no safe threshold of consumption—a view also espoused by the American Temperance Society in the 1840s and the Anti-Saloon League early in [the twentieth] century. The OSAP also evaluated information on alcohol and drugs intended for distribution to schools and communities. It asserted that "materials recommending a designated driver should be rated unacceptable. They encourage heavy alcohol use by implying it is okay to drink to intoxication as long as you don't drive."

Another example of changing attitudes is the history of beliefs about alcohol's effects on fetal development. In the early 1930s, after Prohibition had ended, Charles R. Stockard of Cornell University, a leading authority on embryology, published animal studies that suggested minimal effects on fetal development. At about the same time, Harold T. Hyman of the Columbia University College of Physicians and Surgeons reviewed human experiments and found that "the habitual use of alcohol in moderate amounts by the normal human adult appears to be without any permanent organic effect deleterious in character."

Fetal Alcohol Syndrome

Then, in the 1970s, researchers at the University of Washington described what they called fetal alcohol syndrome, a set of physical and mental abnormalities in children born to women who imbibed during pregnancy. At first, the syndrome appeared to require very heavy consumption, but after further investigation these researchers have come to assert that even a tiny amount of alcohol can cause the disorder. Drinks consumed at the earliest stage of embryonic development, when a woman may have no idea that she is pregnant, can be a particularly potent teratogen [cause of birth defects]. Since 1989, all alcoholic beverages must bear a warning label for pregnant women from the U.S. Surgeon General's office.

Societal reaction to these findings has resulted in strong condemnation of women who drink any alcohol at all while pregnant. In a celebrated Seattle case in 1991, a woman nine months and a couple of weeks pregnant (who had abstained from alcohol during that time) decided to have a drink with her meal in a restaurant. Most embryologists agree that a single drink at such a late stage of pregnancy produces minimal risk. The waiters, however, repeatedly cautioned her against it; she became angry; the waiters lost their jobs. When the story became known, letters appeared in a local newspaper

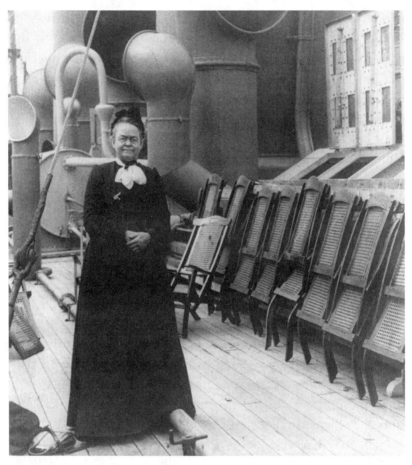

Temperance crusader Carry Nation (1846–1933) destroyed saloons with what became her trademark, a hatchet. Library of Congress.

questioning her fitness as a mother. One University of Washington embryology expert even suggested that pregnant women should no longer be served alcohol in public.

The current worry over the effect of small amounts of alcohol during pregnancy is particularly interesting because belief in alcohol's ability to damage the fetus is a hallmark of American temperance movements in this and the past century. Indeed, as far back as 1726, during the English "gin epidemic," the College of Physicians of London issued a formal warning that parents drinking spirits were committing "a great and growing evil which was, too often, a cause of weak, feeble, and distempered children." There is little question that fetal alcohol syndrome is a real phenomenon, but the explosion in diagnosed cases in conjunction with changing social attitudes merits closer scrutiny.

The First Temperance Movement

Like today's antialcohol movement, earlier campaigns started with temperance and only later began pushing abstinence. In 1785 Benjamin Rush of Philadelphia, celebrated physician and inveterate reformer, became America's most prominent advocate of limited alcohol use. Tens of thousands of copies of his booklet, *An Inquiry into the Effects of Ardent Spirits upon the Human Mind and Body*, were distributed throughout the young nation. Like many of his compatriots, Rush censured spirits while accepting the beneficent effects of milder beverages. His "moral thermometer" introduced a striking visual tool to illustrate the graduated effects of beer and wine (health and wealth) and spirits (intemperance, vice and disease). When reformers "took the pledge" in the early years of the 19th century, it was a pledge to abstain from distilled spirits, not all alcoholic beverages.

The same kind of distinction had been made almost a century earlier in England, during an antispirits crusade in response to the gin epidemic. Rapidly increasing consumption of cheap distilled spirits swamped London during the first half of the 18th century. Gin was blamed for a dramatic rise in deaths and a falling birth rate. [Artist] William Hogarth's powerful prints *Gin Lane* and *Beer Street* were designed to contrast the desolation caused by gin with the healthy prosperity enjoyed by beer drinkers.

Despite the exhortations of Rush and others, until the 1830s most Americans believed that strong alcoholic drinks imparted vitality and health, easing hard work, warding off fevers and other illnesses, and relieving colds and snakebite. Soldiers and sailors took a daily ration of rum, and whiskey had a ceremonial role for marking any social event from a family gathering to an ordination. Even as concern grew, so did the distilling business. Annual consumption peaked around 1830 at an estimated 7.1 gallons of alcohol per adult.

Total Abstention

The creation of the Massachusetts Society for the Suppression of Intemperance in 1812 heralded the first organized antidrinking crusade on a state level. Through the inspiration and determination of one of the most dynamic writers and speakers of the century, the Reverend Lyman Beecher, the tide began to turn in earnest. That same year the annual meeting of the Connecticut Congregational Church received a report on the enormous rise in drinking and concluded, regretfully, that nothing could be done about it. An outraged Beecher demanded that a new report be written, then produced one himself overnight. He called for a crusade against alcohol. In 1826 Beecher limned the specifics of his argument in his epochal *Six Sermons on Intemperance.*

Beecher's words swept hundreds of thousands into America's first temperance movement. One of his signal contributions was to throw out compromise—how can you compromise with a poison? He extended the condemnation of spirits to all alcohol-containing beverages and denounced "prudent use."

"It is not enough," Beecher declaimed, "to erect the flag ahead, to mark the spot where the drunkard dies. It must be planted at the entrance of his course, proclaiming in waving capitals—THIS IS THE WAY TO DEATH!!" Beecher's argument that abstinence is the inevitable final stage of temperance gradually won dominance. In 1836 the American Temperance Society (founded in 1826) officially changed its definition of temperance to abstinence.

A Brief Look at Prohibition

The 18th Amendment to the Constitution—passed by Congress in 1917, and ratified by 3/4 of states by 1919—prohibited the manufacture or sale of alcoholic beverages within the boundaries of the United States.

The Volstead Act of 1919, also known as the National Prohibition Enforcement Act, gave the 18th Amendment some teeth. It clearly defined an alcoholic beverage as one with an alcoholic content greater than 0.5 percent.

The 21st Amendment, which was ratified in 1933, repealed the 18th Amendment. In order to get around the traditional process of ratification by the state legislatures—many of which were expected to vote "dry"—Congress instead called for ratifying conventions in each state. At the completion of delegates' voting, the national count in favor of repeal of the 18th Amendment was 73%.

Stanley K. Schultz, William P. Tishler, "Lecture 17:
The Politics of Prohibition: The 1920s,"
University of Wisconsin, Madison, Dept. of History,
Am. History 102 on-line course,
http://us.history.wisc.edu/hist102/

Not until 1851 did Maine pass its groundbreaking prohibition law, but after that, things moved quickly. By 1855 about a third of Americans lived under democratically achieved laws that prohibited the sale of alcohol. Alcohol consumption fell to less than a third of its pretemperance level and has never again reached the heights of the early republic.

The Woman's Crusade

As the first temperance movement was reaching its peak, another moral debate claimed national attention: slavery. Proabstinence forces began to lose their political strength, especially during the Civil War, when the federal government raised money by means of an excise tax on liquor. Starting in the 1860s, some states repealed their prohibitions, courts in others found the statutes unconstitutional, and prohibition laws in yet other states and territories fell into disuse.

Nevertheless, important antialcohol events continued. The most dramatic, the Woman's Crusade, began in Ohio in 1873. Large groups gathered and employed hymn singing and prayers to sway onlookers against saloons. Out of this movement evolved the Women's Christian Temperance Union (WCTU). Although it is now associated only with prohibition in the popular mind, during the union's prime it pushed for far broader reforms: its platform included equal legal rights for women, the right of women to vote, the institution of kindergartens and an attack on tobacco smoking.

Opposition to alcohol legitimized women's participation in national political life. Because women had been relegated to defense of the home, they could reasonably argue that they had a duty to oppose alcohol and saloons—which were efficiently separating men from their paychecks and turning them into drunken menaces to their families.

In each era of reform, people have tried to influence the education of children and to portray alcohol in a new, presumably more correct light. Today the federal Center for Substance Abuse Prevention (CSAP, the successor to the OSAP) works through prevention materials distributed to schools, but the champion of early efforts was the WCTU's Department of Scientific Temperance Instruction. It successfully fought for mandatory temperance lessons in the public schools and oversaw the writing of approved texts. Pupils would learn, among other things, that "the majority of beer drinkers die of dropsy"; "when alcohol passes down the throat it burns off the skin, leaving it bare and burning"; and "alcohol clogs the brain and turns the liver quickly from yellow to green to black."

The Beginning of National Prohibition

The WCTU's multifarious agenda hampered its effectiveness, though, and in 1895 national leadership of the antialcohol movement was seized by the Anti-Saloon League, which went on to become the most successful single-issue group in American history. At first, the new organization had as its ostensible goal only abolition of the saloon, a social cesspool that had already elicited wide public outcry. As sentiment against alcohol escalated, however, so did the league's intentions, and finally it aimed at national prohibition.

In 1917, aided by a more general national push for health and fitness, what would become the 18th Amendment passed in both houses of Congress by a two-thirds majority. Two years later it became part of the Constitution, coming into effect in January 1920. In the span of one generation, antialcohol campaigns had reached a point where prohibition seemed reasonable to a political majority of Americans. Although brewers and vintners had attempted to portray their products as wholesome, they could not escape the rising tide against intoxicating beverages of any kind.

The first temperance movement had rallied a broad segment of society alarmed at excessive drinking of spirits; only later did the concern move to alcohol in general. Similarly, this second temperance movement initially focused on that widely criticized feature of urban life, the saloon, and then gradually took aim at all drinking.

The Great Experiment

Prohibition lasted almost 14 years. On the positive side, the incidence of liver cirrhosis reached an all-time low: the death rate from the condition fell to half its 1907 peak and did not start to increase again until the amendment was repealed. On the negative side, Prohibition was a blatant failure at permanently convincing a large majority of Americans that alcohol was intrinsically destructive, and it made a significant contribution to the growth of already entrenched criminal organizations. These factors—combined after 1929 with the specious hope that revival of the alcoholic beverage industry would help lift the nation out of the Great Depression—all brought about the overwhelming national rejection of Prohibition in 1933.

As we look at the ways in which the U.S. has addressed issues related to alcohol, we might ask whether prohibition is the inevitable—if brief—culmination of temperance movements. Is our Puritan tradition of uncompromising moral stances still supplying righteous energy to the battle against alcohol? During the 1920s, when many nations of the Western world turned against alcohol, a sustained campaign in the Netherlands led by the workers' movement and religious groups reduced alcohol consumption by 1930 to a very low level, but without legal prohibition. Likewise in Britain: the antialcohol movement reduced consumption even though it did not result in legal bans. Apparently, each nation has its own style of control.

Underlying the U.S. travail with alcohol is the persistence of a sharp dichotomy in the way we perceive it: alcohol is either very good or very bad. Those who oppose alcohol doubt that it might have any value in the diet; those who support it deny any positive effect of prohibition. Compromise seems unthinkable for either side.

Seeking a Workable Stance on Alcohol

Dealing with alcohol on a practical level while maintaining either a totally favorable or totally condemnatory attitude is fraught with trouble. The backlash to prohibition made discussion of the ill effects associated with alcohol extremely difficult, because those worried about drinking problems would often be labeled as straitlaced prudes. Not until another 50 years had passed and new generations had emerged did grassroots movements such as RID and MADD arise and, without apology, promote new laws against drinking. Yet public acceptance of such restrictions on alcohol consumption has a natural limit that can be exceeded only with great danger to the temperance movement itself: that is the lesson of Prohibition.

During the past 15 years, groups such as RID, MADD and the CSAP, aided by advances in medical understanding, have been transforming the image of alcohol into a somber picture heretofore unknown to the current cohort of Americans. This reframing may bring about a healthy rebalancing of our perception of alcohol. But how far will this trend go?

Can we find a stance toward drink that will be workable in the long term? Or will we again achieve an extreme but unsustainable position that will create a lengthy, destructive backlash? There are some signs of moderation—in particular, recent pronouncements by the U.S. Department of Agriculture that it should be considered permission for men and women to consume a glass of wine a day to reduce their risk of heart disease—but it is still unclear whether the U.S. will be able to apply history's lessons.

The Sale of Alcohol Must Be Prohibited

Richmond P. Hobson

In this selection Richmond P. Hobson, a congressman from Alabama, argues in favor of a prohibition amendment in the U.S. House of Representatives on December 22, 1914. Science, he says, proves that widespread, moderate use of alcohol harms society far more than drunkenness does, that fermented liquor is vastly more harmful than distilled spirits, and that the use of alcohol led to the destruction of past civilizations. Hobson also argues that banning the sale of alcohol does not interfere with individual liberty, because the amendment prohibits only its sale, leaving men free to produce or drink alcohol in their homes. Calling alcohol a habit-forming poison, he says its use increases the craving for alcohol and makes its victims slaves of the liquor industry. In arguments that reflect the racist attitudes of his era, Hobson says that alcohol use leads to savage, brutish behavior. He concludes that the cure for the problem is the enactment of a constitutional amendment banning the sale of alcohol. Richmond P. Hobson served as an Alabama representative to Congress from 1907 through 1915.

What is the object of this resolution? It is to destroy the agency that debauches the youth of the land and thereby perpetuates its hold upon the Nation. How does the resolution propose to destroy this agent? In the simplest manner. . . . It does not coerce any drinker. It simply says that barter and sale, matters that have been a public function from the semicivilized days of society, shall not continue the debauching of the youth. Now, the Liquor Trust are wise enough to know that they cannot perpetuate their sway by depending on debauching grown people, so they go to an organic method

Richmond P. Hobson, Testimony Before Congress, December 22, 1914.

of teaching the young to drink. Now we apply exactly the same method to destroy them. We do not try to force old drinkers to stop drinking, but we do effectively put an end to the systematic, organized debauching of our youth through thousands and tens of thousands of agencies throughout the land. Men here may try to escape the simplicity of this problem. They cannot. Some are trying to defend alcohol by saying that its abuse only is bad and that its temperate use is all right. Science absolutely denies it, and proclaims that drunkenness does not produce one-tenth part of the harm to society that the widespread, temperate, moderate drinking does. Some say it is adulteration that harms. Some are trying to say that it is only distilled liquors that do harm. Science comes in now and says that all alcohol does harm; that the malt and fermented liquors produce vastly more harm than distilled liquors, and that it is the general public use of such drinks that has entailed the gradual decline and degeneracy of the nations of the past.

[Those against prohibition] have no foundation in scientific truth to stand upon, and so they resort to all kinds of devious methods.

Their favorite contention is that we cannot reach the evil because of our institutions. This assumes that here is something very harmful and injurious to the public health and morals that imperils our very institutions themselves and the perpetuity of the Nation, but the Nation has not within itself, because of its peculiar organization, the power to bring about the public good and end a great public wrong. They invoke the principle of State rights. As a matter of fact, we are fighting more consistently for State rights than they ever dreamed of. We know the States have the right to settle this question, and furthermore our confidence in three-quarters of all the States to act wisely does not lead us to fear that if we submit the proposition to them they might establish an imperialistic empire. We believe that three-quarters of all the States have the wisdom as well as the right to settle the national prohibition question for this country.

Neither can they take refuge about any assumed question of individual liberty. We do not say that a man shall not drink. We ask for no sumptuary action [regulating behavior on moral grounds]. We do not say that a man shall not have or make liquor in his own home for his own use. Nothing of that sort is involved in this resolution. We only touch the sale. A man may feel he has a right to drink, but he certainly has no inherent right to sell liquor. A man's liberties are absolutely secure in this resolution. The liberties and sanctity of the home are protected. The liberties of the community are secure, the liberties of the county are secure, and the liberties of the State are secure.

The Right of States to Be Dry

Let no one imagine that a State to-day has the real power and right to be wet of its own volition. Under the taxing power of the Federal Government by act of Congress, Congress could make every State in the country dry. They need not think it is an inherent right for a State to be wet; it is not; but there is an inherent right in every State and every county and every township to be dry, and these rights are now trampled upon, and this monster prides himself in trampling upon them.

Why, here to-day Member after Member [of Congress] has proclaimed that prohibition does not prohibit, and I have heard them actually tell us that prohibition could not prohibit. They tell us that this interstate liquor power is greater than the National Government. . . .

I say now, as I said before, I will meet this foe on a hundred battlefields. If the Sixty-third Congress does not grant this plain right of the people for this referendum to change their organic law, to meet this mighty evil, the Sixty-fourth Congress will be likewise invoked. I do not say that we are going to get a two-thirds majority here tonight . . . because we have not yet had a chance to appeal to Caesar: but I do say that the day is coming when we shall have that referendum sent to the States, nor is that day as far distant as some may imagine. Unless this question has been made a State matter, as we are asking now for it to be so made by being removed from national politics, and referred to the States—if this is not done by the intervening Congresses, I here announce to you the determination of the great moral, the great spiritual, the great temperance and prohibition forces of this whole Nation to make this question the paramount issue in 1916, not only to gain a two-thirds majority in the Houses of Congress, but to have an administration that neither in the open nor under cover will fight this reform, so that in the spring of 1917 with an extraordinary session of the Sixty-fifth Congress we will have a command from the masters of men and of Congress to grant this right to the people. My appeal is to each one of you now, be a man when the vote is taken and do your duty.

Alcohol Is a Habit-Forming Poison

Alcohol has the property of chloroform and ether of penetrating actually into the nerve fibers themselves, putting the tissues under an anesthetic which prevents pain at first, but when the anesthetic effect is over discomfort follows throughout the tissues of the whole body, particularly the nervous system, which causes a craving for relief by recourse to the very substance that produced the disturbance. This craving grows directly with the amount and regularity of the drinking.

The poisoning attack of alcohol is specially severe in the cortex cerebrum—the top part of the brain—where resides the center of inhibition, or of will power, causing partial paralysis, which liberates lower activities otherwise held in control, causing a man to be more of a brute, but to imagine that he has been stimulated, when he is really partially paralyzed.

This center of inhibition is the seat of the will power, which of necessity declines a little in strength every time partial paralysis takes place.

Thus a man is [a] little less of a man after each drink he takes. In this way continued drinking causes a progressive weakening of the will and a progressive growing of the craving, so that after a time, if persisted in, there must come a point where the will power cannot control the craving and the victim is in the grip of the habit.

When the drinking begins young the power of the habit becomes overwhelming, and the victim might as well have shackles. It is estimated that there are 5,000,000 heavy drinkers and drunkards in America, and these men might as well have a ball and chain on their ankles, for they are more abject slaves than those black men who were driven by slave drivers.

These victims are driven imperatively to procure their liquor, no matter at what cost. A few thousand brewers and distillers, making up the organizations composing the great Liquor Trust, have a monopoly of the supply, and they therefore own these 5,000,000 slaves and through them they are able to collect two and one-half billions of dollars cash from the American people every year.

Liquor Destroys the Character of Men

The first finding of science that alcohol is a protoplasmic poison and the second finding that it is an insidious, habit-forming drug, though of great importance, are as unimportant when compared with the third finding, that alcohol degenerates the character of men and tears down their spiritual nature. Like the other members of the group of oxide derivatives of hydrocarbons, alcohol is not only a general poison, but it has a chemical affinity or deadly appetite for certain particular tissues. Strychnine tears down the spinal cord. Alcohol tears down the top part of the brain in a man, attacks certain tissues in an animal, certain cells in a flower. It has been established that whatever the line of a creature's evolution alcohol will attack that line. Every type and every species is evolving in building from generation to generation along some particular line. Man is evolving in the top part of the brain, the seat of the will power, the seat of the moral senses, and of the spiritual nature, the recognition of right and wrong, the consciousness of God and of duty and of brotherly love and of self-sacrifice.

Liquor Makes Men Savages

All life in the universe is founded upon the principle of evolution. Alcohol directly reverses that principle. Man has risen from the savage up through successive steps to the level of the semisavage, the semicivilized, and the highly civilized.

Liquor promptly degenerates the red man, throws him back into savagery. It will promptly put a tribe on the war path.

Liquor will actually make a brute out of a negro, causing him to commit unnatural crimes.

The effect is the same on the white man, though the white man being further evolved it takes longer time to reduce him to the same level. Starting young, however, it does not take a very long time to speedily cause a man in the forefront of civilization to pass through the successive stages and become semicivilized, semisavage, savage, and, at last, below the brute.

The Great Tragedy

The spiritual nature of man gives dignity to his life above the life of the brute. It is this spiritual nature of man that makes him in the image of his Maker, so that the Bible referred to man as being a little lower than the angels. It is a tragedy to blight the physical life. No measure can be made of blighting the spiritual life.

Nature does not tolerate reversing its evolutionary principle, and proceeds automatically to exterminate any creature,

103

any animal, any race, any species that degenerates. Nature adopts two methods of extermination—one to shorten the life, the other to blight the offspring.

Science has thus demonstrated that alcohol is a protoplasmic poison, poisoning all living things; that alcohol is a habit-forming drug that shackles millions of our citizens and maintains slavery in our midst; that it lowers in a fearful way the standard of efficiency of the Nation, reducing enormously the national wealth, entailing startling burdens of taxation, encumbering the public with the care of crime, pauperism, and insanity; that it corrupts politics and public servants, corrupts the Government, corrupts the public morals, lowers terrifically the average standard of character of the citizenship, and undermines the liberties and institutions of the Nation; that it undermines and blights the home and the family, checks education, attacks the young when they are entitled to protection, undermines the public health, slaughtering, killing, and wounding our citizens many-fold times more than war, pestilence, and famine combined; that it blights the progeny of the Nation, flooding the land with a horde of degenerates; that it strikes deadly blows at the life of the Nation itself and at the very life of the race, reversing the great evolutionary principles of nature and the purposes of the Almighty.

Prohibition Must Be Placed in the Constitution

There can be but one verdict, and that is this great destroyer must be destroyed. The time is ripe for fulfillment. The present generation, the generation to which we belong, must cut this millstone of degeneracy from the neck of humanity. . . .

To cure this organic disease we must have recourse to the organic law. The people themselves must act upon this question. A generation must be prevailed upon to place prohibition in their own constitutional law, and such a generation could be counted upon to keep it in the Constitution during its lifetime. The Liquor Trust of necessity would disintegrate. The youth would grow up sober. The final, scientific conclusion is that we must have constitutional prohibition, prohibiting only the sale, the manufacture for sale, and everything that pertains to the sale, and invoke the power of both Federal and State Governments for enforcement. The resolution is drawn to fill these requirements.

Prohibition Is Wrong

Percy Andreae

In the following selection, first published in 1915, Percy Andreae argues against the imposition of laws prohibiting the sale of alcohol. Andreae claims it is wrong to ban all sales of alcohol because some people misuse the drink. He also asserts that only a few prohibitionists sincerely want to end abusive drinking. Most, he writes, have a hidden agenda: to impose their religious beliefs on others. He argues that prohibitionists seek to make the sale of liquor, not its purchase or consumption, a crime because they would lose popular support if they tried to stop all liquor drinking. Their underlying goal, he says, is the imposition of an extreme and mirthless form of religion. Andreae argues that prohibition endangers civilized society with its imposition of narrow beliefs and religious intolerance. A well-known spokesman against prohibition in the early twentieth century, Percy Andreae organized successful opposition to the temperance movement, including resistance to the Ohio Anti-Saloon League after its sweeping victories in the state elections in 1908.

Somewhere in the Bible it is said: "If thy right hand offend thee, cut it off." I used to think the remedy somewhat radical. But to-day, being imbued with the wisdom of the prohibitionist, I have to acknowledge that, if the Bible in general, and that passage in it in particular, has a fault, it lies in its ultraconservativeness. What? Merely cut off my own right hand if it offend me? What business have my neighbors to keep their right hands if I am not able to make mine behave itself? Off with the lot of them! Let there be no right hands; then I am certain that mine won't land me in trouble.

I have met many active prohibitionists, both in this and in other countries, all of them thoroughly in earnest. In some in-

Percy Andreae, "A Glimpse Behind the Mask of Prohibition," *The Prohibition Movement in Its Broader Bearings upon Our Social, Commercial, and Religious Liberties.* Chicago: Felix Mendelsohn, 1915.

stances I have found that their allegiance to the cause of prohibition took its origin in the fact that some near relative or friend had succumbed to over-indulgence in liquor. In one or two cases the man himself had been a victim of this weakness, and had come to the conclusion, firstly that every one else was constituted as he was, and, therefore, liable to the same danger; and secondly, that unless every one were prevented from drinking, he would not be secure from the temptation to do so himself.

Religious Zealots Seek Political Power

This is one class of prohibitionists. The other, and by far the larger class, is made up of religious zealots, to whom prohibition is a word having at bottom a far wider application than that which is generally attributed to it. The liquor question, if there really is such a question per se, is merely put forth by them as a means to an end, an incidental factor in a fight which has for its object the supremacy of a certain form of religious faith. The belief of many of these people is that the Creator frowns upon enjoyment of any and every kind, and that he has merely endowed us with certain desires and capacities for pleasure in order to give us an opportunity to please Him by resisting them. They are, of course, perfectly entitled to this belief, though some of us may consider it eccentric and somewhat in the nature of a libel on the Almighty. But are they privileged to force that belief on all their fellow beings? That, in substance, is the question that is involved in the present-day prohibition movement.

For it is all nonsense to suppose that because, perhaps, one in a hundred or so of human beings is too weak to resist the temptation of over-indulging in drink—for of over-indulging in anything else, for the matter of that—therefore all mankind is going to forego the right to indulge in that enjoyment in moderation. The leaders of the so-called prohibition movement know as well as you and I do that you can no more prevent an individual from taking a drink if he be so inclined than you can prevent him from scratching himself if he itches. They object to the existence of the saloon, not, bear in mind, to that of the badly conducted saloon, but to that of the well-regulated, decent saloon, and wherever they succeed in destroying the latter, their object, which is the manifestation of their political power, is attained. That for every decent, well-ordered saloon they destroy, there springs up a dive, or speak-easy, or blind tiger, or whatever other name it may be known by, and the dispensing of drink continues as merrily as before, doesn't disturb them at all. They make the sale of liquor a crime, but steadily refuse to make its purchase and consumption an offense. Time and again the industries affected by this apparently senseless crusade have endeavored to have laws passed making dry territories really dry by providing for the punishment of the man who buys drink as well as the man who sells it. But every such attempt has been fiercely opposed by the prohibition leaders. And why? Because they know only too well that the first attempt to really prohibit drinking would put an end to their power forever. They know that 80 per cent of those who, partly by coercion, partly from sentiment, vote dry, are perfectly willing to restrict the right of the remaining 20 per cent to obtain drink, but that they are not willing to sacrifice that right for themselves.

Prohibition's True Goal

And so the farce called prohibition goes on, and will continue to go on as long as it brings grist to the mill of the managers who are producing it. But the farce conceals something far more serious than that which is apparent to the public on the face of it. Prohibition is merely the title of the movement. Its real purpose is of a religious, sectarian character, and this applies not only to the movement in America, but to the same movement in England, a fact which, strangely enough, has rarely, if at all, been recognized by those who have dealt with the question in the public press.

If there is any one who doubts the truth of this statement, let me put this to him: How many Roman Catholics are prohibitionists? How many Jews, the most temperate race on earth, are to be found in the ranks of prohibition? Or Lutherans? Or German Protestants generally? What is the proportion of Episcopalians to that of Methodists, Baptists and Presbyterians, and the like, in the active prohibition army? The answer to these questions will, I venture to say, prove conclusively the assertion that the fight for prohibition is synonymous with the fight of a certain religious sect, or group of religious sects, for the supremacy of its ideas. In England it is the Nonconformists, which is in that country the generic name for the same sects, who are fighting the fight, and the suppression of liquor there is no more the ultimate end they have in view than it is here in America. It is the fads and restrictions that are part and parcel of their lugubrious notion of God-worship which they eventually hope to impose upon the rest of humanity; a Sunday without a smile, no games, no recreation, no pleasures, no music, card-playing tabooed, dancing anathematized, the beauties of art decried as impure—in short, this world reduced to a barren, forbidding wilderness in which we, its inhabitants, are to pass our time contemplating the joys of the next. Rather problematical joys, by the way, if we are to suppose we shall worship God in the next world in the same somber way as we are called upon by these worthies to do in this.

Knowledge Leads to Health

To my mind, and that of many others, the hearty, happy laugh of a human being on a sunny Sunday is music sweeter to the ears of that being's Creator than all the groaning and moanings, and *misericordias* [cries for mercy] that rise to heaven from the lips of those who would deprive us altogether of the faculty and the privilege of mirth. That some overdo hilarity and become coarse and offensive, goes without saying. There are people without the sense of proportion or propriety in all matters. Yet none of us think of abolishing pleasures because a few do not know how to enjoy them in moderation and with decency, and become an offense to their neighbors.

The drink evil has existed from time immemorial, just as sexual excess has, and all other vices to which mankind is and always will be more or less prone, though less in proportion as education progresses and the benefits of civilization increased. Sexual excess, curiously enough, has never interested our hyper-religious friends, the prohibitionists, in anything like the degree that the vice of excessive drinking does. Perhaps this is because the best of us have our pet aversions and our pet weaknesses. Yet this particular vice has produced more evil results to the human race than all other vices combined, and, in spite of it, mankind, thanks not to prohibitive laws and restrictive legislation, but to the forward strides of knowledge and to patient and intelligent education, is to-day ten times sounder in body and healthier in mind than it ever was in the world's history.

Now, if the habit of drinking to excess were a growing one, as our prohibitionist friends claim that it is, we should to-day, instead of discussing this question with more or less intelligence, not be here at all to argue it; for the evil, such as it is, has existed for so many ages that, if it were as general and as contagious as is claimed, and its results as far-reaching as they are painted, the human race would have been destroyed by it long ago. Of course, the contrary is the case. The world has progressed in this as in all other respects. Compare, for instance, the drinking to-day with the drinking of a thousand years ago, nay, of only a hundred odd years ago, when a man, if he wanted to ape his so-called betters, did so by contriving to be carried to bed every night "drunk as a lord." Has that condition of affairs been altered by legislative measures restricting the right of the individual to control himself? No. It has been altered by that far greater power, the moral force of education and the good example which teaches mankind the very thing that prohibition would take from it: the virtue of self-control and moderation in all things.

Prohibition Nullifies Self-Control

And here we come to the vital distinction between the advocacy of temperance and the advocacy of prohibition. Temperance and self-control are convertible [interchangeable] terms. Prohibition, or that which it implies, is the direct negation of the term self-control. In order to save the small percentage of men who are too weak to resist their animal desires, it aims to put chains on every man, the weak and the strong alike. And if this is proper in one respect, why not in all respects? Yet, what would one think of a proposition to keep all men locked up because a certain number have a propensity to steal? Theoretically, perhaps, all crime or vice could be stopped by chaining us all up as we chain up a wild animal, and only allowing us to take exercise under proper supervision and control. But while such a measure would check crime, it would not eliminate the criminal. It is true, some people are only kept from vice and crime by the fear of punishment. Is not, indeed, the basis of some men's religiousness nothing else but the fear of Divine punishment? The doctrines of certain religious denominations not entirely unknown in the prohibition camp make self-respect, which is the foundation of self-control and of all morality, a sin. They decry rather than advocate it. They love to call themselves miserable, helpless sinners, cringing before the flaming sword, and it is the flaming sword, not the exercise of their own enlightened will, that keeps them within decent bounds. Yet has this fear of eternal punishment contributed one iota toward the intrinsic betterment of the human being? If it had, would so many of our Christian creeds have discarded it, admitting that it is the precepts of religion, not its dark and dire threats, that make men truly better and stronger within themselves to resist that which our self-respect

Law enforcement officials, government officials, and concerned citizens regularly destroyed barrels of liquor and beer to keep alcohol out of circulation during Prohibition-era raids on saloons. Library of Congress.

teaches us is bad and harmful? The growth of self-respect in man, with its outward manifestation, self-control, is the growth of civilization. If we are to be allowed to exercise it no longer, it must die in us from want of nutrition, and men must become savages once more, fretting now at their chains, which they will break as inevitably as the sun will rise to-morrow and herald a new day.

I consider the danger which threatens civilized society from the growing power of a sect whose views on prohibition are merely an exemplification of their general low estimate of man's ability to rise to higher things—by his own volition to be of infinitely greater consequence than the danger that, in putting their narrow theories to the test, a few billions of invested property will be destroyed, a number of great wealth-producing industries wiped out, the rate of individual taxation largely increased, and a million or so of struggling wage earners doomed to face starvation. These latter considerations, of course, must appeal to every thinking man, but what are they compared with the greater questions involved? Already the government of our State, and indeed of a good many other States, has passed practically into the hands of a few preacher-politicians of a certain creed. With the machine they have built up, by appealing to the emotional weaknesses of the more or less unintelligent masses, they have lifted themselves on to a pedestal of power that has enabled them to dictate legislation or defeat it at their will, to usurp the functions of the governing head of the State and actually induce him to delegate to them the appointive powers vested in him by the Constitution. When a Governor elected by the popular vote admits, as was recently the case, that he can not appoint a man to one of the most important offices of the State without the indorsement of the irresponsible leader of a certain semi-religious movement, and when he submits to this same personage for correction and amendment his recommendation to the legislative body, there can scarcely be any doubt left in any reasonable mind as to the extent of the power wielded by this leader, or as to the uses he and those behind him intend putting it to.

Government by Emotion or by Reason?

And what does it all mean? It means that government by emotion is to be substituted for government by reason, and government by emotion, of which history affords many examples, is, according to the testimony of all ages, the most dangerous and pernicious of all forms of government. It has already crept into the legislative assemblies of most of the States of the Union, and is being craftily fostered by those who know how easily it can be made available for their purposes—purposes to the furtherance of which cool reason would never lend itself. Prohibition is but one of its fruits, and the hand that is plucking this fruit is the same hand of intolerance that drove forth certain of our forefathers from the land of their birth to seek the sheltering freedom of these shores.

What a strange reversal of conditions! The intolerants of a few hundred years ago are the upholders of liberty to-day, while those they once persecuted, having multiplied by grace of the very liberty that has so long sheltered them here, are now planning to impose the tyranny of their narrow creed upon the descendants of their persecutors of yore. Let the greater public, which is, after all, the arbiter of the country's destinies, pause and ponder these things before they are allowed to progress too far. Prohibition, though it must cause, and is already causing, incalculable damage, may never succeed in this country; but that which is behind it, as the catapults and the cannon were behind the battering rams in the battles of olden days, is certain to succeed unless timely measures of prevention are resorted to; and if it does succeed, we shall witness the enthronement of a monarch in this land of liberty compared with whose autocracy the autocracy of the Russian Czar is a mere trifle.

The name of this monarch is Religious Intolerance.

Alcohol Use and Abuse Among American Indians

Jerrold E. Levy

In this selection Jerrold E. Levy describes how North American Indians in the western United States learned to drink alcohol from frontiersmen who binged on enormous quantities. When most of the nation drastically decreased drinking after national prohibition, Native Americans, isolated on Indian reservations, continued to binge. Levy also states that although it is commonly claimed that Native Americans in the late 20th century died from alcoholism at about five times the overall rate for America, this statistic may be biased. He explains that researchers studying Indian reservations typically have lumped together deaths from causes that may not have been alcohol related, including homicide, suicide, and accidents, with deaths resulting directly from alcohol, such as cirrhosis of the liver. Levy questions whether this practice leads to accurate results. Also, most investigators have not distinguished between tribal groups in their studies, obscuring significant differences. Nevertheless, Levy explains, the binge drinking common in some Native American cultures can be labeled alcoholism by most measures. He also expresses hope that more careful research will lead to more effective prevention and treatment programs in the future. Jerrold E. Levy, a professor of anthropology at the University of Arizona, has written extensively on the Navajo people and drinking practices among American Indians.

The "drunken Indian" has been a subject of continuing concern in the United States from the earliest contacts between Europeans and Indians down to the present day. Popular notions about the nature of alcohol and excessive drinking,

Jerrold E. Levy, "Alcoholism, Indian," *Encyclopedia of North American Indians.* New York: Houghton Mifflin, 1996. Reproduced by permission of Houghton Mifflin Company.

however, have changed radically over the years. During the seventeenth and eighteenth centuries it was thought that the "savage" nature of Indians was expressed without inhibitions under the effects of alcohol. From the nineteenth century until the present, the idea that Indians are physiologically unable to handle alcohol as well as white Americans has become increasingly popular and is, indeed, a belief subscribed to by many Indians themselves. On the other hand, most contemporary studies of American Indians attribute deviant behaviors such as alcohol abuse to social disorganization and the stress of acculturation. A number of deprivations, including confinement to reservations and federal wardship, are cited as causes for many Indians to feel inadequate. Alcohol, according to this view, has been the easiest and quickest way to deaden the senses and to forget the feeling of inadequacy.

With few exceptions, the Indians of America north of Mexico had no knowledge of alcohol prior to contact with Europeans. In consequence, the drinking behaviors observed since the nineteenth century can be traced directly to the contact situation. In the Southwest, the Akimel O'odham (Pima), Papago (Tohono O'odham), and River Yuman peoples did make wine from the saguaro cactus as well as from the agave and mesquite. However, the alcoholic content of these beverages was quite low—between 3 and 4 percent—and their nutritional value was significant. Agave wine, for example, was rich in sucrose and vitamins B1 and C. It was also an important source of comparatively safe liquid in areas where drinking water was scarce or contaminated. In the east, the Cherokees and Catawbas made a wine from persimmons.

The Pimas and Papagos made large quantities of saguaro wine in July, following the harvest of the first crops. During a saguaro ceremony all adults drank copiously, believing that, as humans saturated themselves with the wine, so the earth would be saturated with rain. Informal and secular use of alcohol appears to have been relatively infrequent so that, prior to the coming of the Europeans, none of the tribes of America (north of Rio Grande) had a well-developed "drinking ethic" to prepare them for the advent of beverages with high alcoholic content.

It is difficult for the contemporary reader to fully appreciate the drinking practices in the United States during the nineteenth century. We are apt to compare descriptions of early drinking by Indians or frontiersmen with the more familiar drinking habits of the urbanized, largely middle-class society of the late twentieth century. The consumption of alcohol in nineteenth-century America, however, was unlike anything twentieth-century Americans are likely to experience in their own lives. Between 1790 and 1840, Americans drank more alcoholic beverages—nearly half a pint of hard liquor per adult male each day—than at any other time in our history. The most popular beverages were cider and whiskey. Water was usually of poor quality, milk was scarce and unsafe, and coffee, tea, and wine were imported and expensive.

Vast Quantities of Liquor on the Frontier

When the frontier moved west of the Appalachians, settlers were cut off from the East and were forced to develop their own markets. Land transportation was too expensive for the bountiful corn crops to be hauled over the mountains. Whiskey was widely produced because it was easily preserved and traded, and it soon became the medium of exchange on the frontier.

During the colonial period there were already two distinct styles of drinking distilled spirits. Many Americans took small amounts of alcohol daily, either alone or with the family at home. "Drams" were taken upon rising, with meals, during midday breaks, and at bedtime. Ingesting frequent but small doses develops a tolerance to the effects of alcohol, and this style of drinking did not generally lead to intoxication. The other style of drinking was the communal binge, a form of public drinking to intoxication, and practically any gathering of three or more men provided an occasion for drinking vast quantities of liquor.

Western Native Americans Learn to Binge

Although consumption declined for the nation as a whole during the latter half of the nineteenth century, binge drinking spread to the western frontier and became an integral part of the periodic gambling, fighting, and whoring sprees engaged in by trappers, miners, soldiers, and cowboys. Thus, western Indians had as tutors some of the heaviest drinkers in the nation at the time of their most disruptive contacts with Anglo-Americans. And Anglo-Americans, for a variety of reasons, encouraged this style of drinking among the western Indians. Fur companies, for example, preferred to pay trappers, white as well as Indian, with liquor rather than money so that they would drink up their profits and be forced to trap the next year. Not only did the Indians learn the binge style of drinking from observing those who introduced liquor to them, they also found the white man's notion that a man was not responsible for actions committed while intoxicated consonant with their own notions of possession by supernatural agents. Supernatural power was obtained in dreams or induced trance states that resembled the intoxicated state. Over the years the nation became increasingly urbanized, and drinking styles changed radically after national prohibition. Drinking on Indian reservations, however, continued largely unchanged due to their relative isolation from the larger society.

Today we are told that Indians and Alaska Natives die from "alcoholism" at almost five times the overall rate for the nation. Such statistics not only give cause for concern but also shape how the problem of Indian drinking is perceived. Moreover, the manner in which the data on Indian drinking is presented reflects our assumptions about the nature of alcohol as well as our image of the American Indian and of ourselves as a people. Because many believe that homicide, suicide, and accidents are strongly associated with alcohol, deaths from these "related" causes are often lumped together with deaths directly the result of drinking, such as alcoholic cirrhosis. But whether this image and our concern are directly related to an objective assessment of the Indians' use of alcohol or to more subtle involvements between whites and Indians is difficult to say.

The populations of most Indian tribes are so small that the relatively small number of occurrences of deaths from alcoholic cirrhosis or suicide will vary widely from year to year. The need to avoid bias caused by these fluctuations and to use population denominators of sufficient size to obtain statistically meaningful results leads most investigators to aggregate data for "all Indians" or Indians of a particular administrative region and to compare them to national averages. These practices, however, obscure the considerable differences in culture, environment, and interethnic relations among the many Indian groups. Obscured also are the considerable differences in mortality rates among regions of the nation as well as rural and urban non-Indian populations.

Drinking Patterns Depend More on Region than Ethnicity

Today the southern states along with those of the Rocky Mountain West have relatively high rates of death from what have come to be thought of as alcohol-related causes, a circumstance often attributed to our frontier heritage. During the 1980s, for example, the average annual age-adjusted mortality rate from "selected alcohol-related causes" for twenty-one northern states was forty-five deaths per 100,000 population. By contrast the eight mountain states averaged sixty-six deaths, a rate nearly 50 percent higher.

In general, urban areas have lower mortality rates from alcohol-related causes than do rural areas, and regional differences are even greater in rural areas because of the persistence of older cultural factors as well as certain environmental variables. When rural areas of the northern and southern mountain region are compared, the northern tier has considerably lower mortality rates than the southern. . . .

Western Indians live almost entirely in rural areas and may be expected to have death rates from alcohol-related causes more in line with those of the rural populations of the states in which they live. This is in fact the case for the Navajo tribe, which is the largest single tribe in the nation. When death rates for cirrhosis, suicide, homicide, and accidents among rural Navajos and Anglos in Arizona were compared, they were found to be virtually the same with the exception of deaths from accidents. There is also evidence to suggest that the proportions of these deaths due to alcohol abuse are virtually the same in the two groups. The higher rate of deaths due to accidents is due to environmental differences rather than to a higher proportion of alcohol-related accidents.

Differences Between Tribes

Tribal differences continue to be large, however, and the situation found among the Navajos cannot be generalized to all tribes. The Pueblos of New Mexico, for example seem to have lower rates of alcohol-related deaths than do rural Anglos, while the tribes of the northern plains appear to have rates higher than those of their non-Indian neighbors.

Statistical data on drinking patterns often fail to reflect the distinctive nature of Indian society. The Indian style of binge drinking would be considered alcoholic by most measures used in studies of the subject. Withdrawal symptoms, generally thought to be a certain sign of physiological addiction, were reported by over 50 percent of drinkers in one study of 67 Navajo men and 45 women conducted from 1966 through 1990. Yet most of these drinkers became abstinent by the time they were thirty-five or forty years of age, a circumstance one would not expect if they had been addicted to alcohol. It seems likely that much of the explanation involves the characteristic style of drinking that takes place in Indian communities. The reservation style of drinking among the Navajos, for example, fosters sudden withdrawal. After ingesting large amounts of alcohol at one time, drinkers most frequently pass out or find their supply exhausted. Especially on reservations, there are no easily available supplies to help a drinker taper off. In towns bordering the reservation, drinkers may get arrested or wake up after drinking with no money. Social and legal prohibitions against drinking, the absence of a ready supply, and the fact that Indians who drink in public or in bars in off-reservation border towns are often arrested all foster sudden withdrawal and, in consequence, a high incidence of hallucinatory experiences.

Alcohol use and abuse is a heterogeneous phenomenon both among and within various tribes, and no global explanation, either racial or social, appears to account for it. As the number of Indian deaths from infectious diseases has decreased over the past thirty years, the Indian Health Service and Indian communities themselves are turning their attention more to the chronic disorders associated with aging as well as to such social pathologies as alcohol abuse. It is to be hoped that this will lead to a better understanding of the phenomenon and ultimately to more effective prevention and treatment programs.

CHAPTER 3

Current Issues in Alcohol Use

The Persistent Problem of Youthful Binge Drinking

Garry Boulard

Although alcohol use among underage youth has decreased over the past twenty years, the number of young people dying from alcohol-related accidents has stayed the same. These deaths are often caused by binge drinking—consuming dangerous amounts of alcohol in a short period of time. In this selection Garry Boulard explores possible reasons for this apparent paradox, including a lack of parental guidance, alcohol advertising, and Internet sites that promote binge drinking. Boulard also discusses possible solutions, including educating young people to drink safely, implementing laws to make it more difficult for underage youth to buy alcohol, and increasing programs that educate high school and college students about the harmful effects of drinking and driving and binge drinking. Garry Boulard is a freelance writer and frequent contributor to State Legislatures *journal.*

The stories have been shocking, abruptly reminding a nation of a problem that remains unsolved: in the last half of 2004, six college-age students in Colorado died as a result of binge drinking.

Although each fatality was different in its circumstance—Samantha Spady, 19, a sophomore at Colorado State University, died after drinking vanilla vodka and more than two dozen beers, while Benett Bertoli, 20, also a CSU student, was found dead on a couch at an off-campus party from a combination of alcohol, methadone and benzodiazepene—the events leading up to the deaths were maddeningly familiar.

In almost every case, the fatalities were the unexpected ending to a boisterous party almost always involving large gatherings of young people on weekend nights consuming prodigious amounts of alcohol, sometimes for two days straight.

The number of Colorado deaths from binge drinking in late 2004 was exceptionally large, but the state is not alone. It killed Thomas Ryan Hauser, 23, a student at Virginia Tech in September. Blake Hammontree, 19, died at his fraternity house at the University of Oklahoma, also in September. Bradley Kemp, 20, died in October at his home near the University of Arkansas, where he was a student. Steven Judd died celebrating his 21st birthday with fraternity friends at New Mexico State University in November.

Alcohol-Related Death Rate Remains Constant

Those deaths did not occur in a vacuum. According to statistics from the National Institute for Alcohol Abuse and Alcoholism, more than 1,400 college students die from alcohol-related deaths each year including motor vehicle crashes. Unfortunately, that number has remained constant even though both high school and college-age drinking has decreased.

"The numbers have been going in the right direction," says Peter Cressey, the president of the Distilled Spirits Council of the United States. "There is today less regular use of alcohol on college campuses than there was 20 years ago. There has been a drop in the number of college students both of age and not of age who drink at all during any given month. And the data for eighth, 10th, and 12th graders who consume alcohol has also shown a downward trend."

But what hasn't changed, industry, health and alcohol experts all agree, is the stubborn number of young people who continue to engage in destructive behavior.

"The issue is not the 30,000 kids on the campus of the University of Colorado, or any other school, who drink legally or illegally, but somehow manage to do it without any great peril," says Ralph Blackman, the president of the Century Council, a not-for-profit organization dedicated to fighting drunk driving and underage drinking.

"The issue is binge drinking and the continuing large numbers of kids who insist on overconsumption to a level that has a very decided risk for a dangerous result," continues Blackman. "That is a phenomenon that very much remains with us."

Out of the Closet

Trying to find a specific reason for the persistence of binge drinking among the young is a subject that both vexes and causes great debate among the nation's policymakers. Do younger people just naturally like to get drunk, or in some cases, very drunk? Is it a matter of upbringing or income? Is it a reflection of a troubled and anxious society? "You could ask questions like that all day, and not really get any solid answers," says Paul Hanson, a professor emeritus of sociology at the State University of New York, Potsdam. "The only thing you could be sure of is that no matter how many different ways we approach it with different solutions, binge drinking continues among the very young, generation after generation."

But some experts believe one thing that is different with those who are a part of what demographers call the Millennials—those born in 1980 or after—and their predecessors, is that binge drinking today is out of the closet and celebrated on almost a worldwide basis due to the Internet.

"There is a huge difference from when many of us went to school in the 1960s and '70s and today," says Stephen Bentley, a coordinator of substance abuse services at the Wardenberg Health Center at the University of Colorado. "Back in our day we really did not want any attention of any kind, we did not want adults of the world to know that we were drinking and partying excessively," continues Bentley. "But today young people who engage in this kind of behavior are actually very proud of what they are doing, they post their own Web sites about their parties so that everyone else can see what they did."

One of the Web sites, called shamings.com, features pictures of drunken young men, updated on a regular basis, sometimes sleeping in their own vomit, often half naked, and many times covered with magic marker salutations alluding to their drinking prowess or lack thereof.

One of the Web site creators, Ricky Van Veen, explained to the *Washington Post* the guidelines used by the Web site in determining whether or not to post a binge drinker's picture: "The standard rule is, if you fall asleep with your shoes on, you're fair game," he said.

Alcohol Ads Appeal to Youth

For Julia Sherman, field director with the Center on Alcohol Marketing and Youth, binge drinking self-promotion is almost a natural outgrowth of what she says is the alcohol industry's "preoccupation with the young."

"The ads that are being put out there today are not your Mom and Pop, 'Mabel, Black Label,' ads of another era, but ads that are very much geared toward an exceedingly young demographic," she says.

"The whole ad focus of the alcohol industry has changed both in tenor and in numbers," says Sherman. "Their Web site ads now feature computer games and premiums for downloading music. They run ads in what are called the 'laddie magazines,' that are edgier than anything adults are seeing in their magazines. It is all part of a non-stop, never-ending pitch for the youth market."

According to a study released by the Center on Alcohol Marketing and Youth [in October 2004], the number of alcohol ads on TV jumped by nearly 90,000 between 2001 and

2003, with some 23 percent of the ads "more likely to be seen by the average underage person for every four seen by the average adult."

Cressey of the Distilled Spirits Council, among other industry leaders, disputes that there has been any concerted targeting of young people, and notes that his group will not permit any member to advertise where the media is not at least a 70/30, adult to minor, demographic.

"We also require through our code that all models in our ads be at least 25 years old," adds Cressey, a requirement that is also generally followed by members of the Beer Institute.

But even working within those parameters, the impact of drinking ads, usually showing young people at a beach party, rap concert, or skate boarding, remains a matter of contention.

Inability to Understand Danger

"The problem is that how we view television has changed greatly in the last generation," says Sherman. "It used to be that there was one TV and the entire family was watching it, which meant that there would probably be some sort of adult filtering or response to whatever the ad message was. But that is much harder today when over 30 percent of kids aged two to eight, and two-thirds over the age of eight, have their own TVs in their own rooms."

The end result may not only be a message received early on that drinking alcohol is attractive, but an actual inability at an age leading all the way up to college to discern alcohol's potential danger. "There is a lot of research out there showing that even up to the age of 21 and beyond a young body is not fully developed and it does not absorb alcohol as well as it might in an older person," says Blackman of the Century Council. "Just as important is the evidence that your brain is not fully developed at that point either, so that issues of risk-taking and behavior are assessed in a different way."

To make matters worse, State University of New York's Hanson says, zero tolerance alcohol programs or efforts to make campuses virtually alcohol-free have a funny way of backfiring. "Prohibition is a classic example of how the laws in these matters can end up being counterproductive by actually making the thing that is being prohibited more attractive. That remains especially true for young people who don't like to be told what not to do.

"And when that happens," says Hanson, "young people very often find themselves involved in these dangerous events centered around heavy episodic drinking, which is the very last thing we want to see happen."

Teaching Moderation

Hanson has also noticed in his own research that the percentage of students who drink tends to decrease as they go from being freshmen to seniors. He says policymakers would be wiser to focus on what he calls "harm reduction policies" that acknowledge young people are going to drink no matter what, but emphasize responsible drinking through education—even to minors.

Similarly Colorado University's Bentley has noticed the effectiveness of the restorative justice approach on many college campuses that require students who have engaged in binge drinking to face the people who suffered the consequences of their behavior when they were drunk.

"That means the neighbors who were trying to study when the party was blaring," says Bentley, "or friends who had to take care of them when they were throwing up all over themselves or were otherwise dead drunk."

Legislatively, some lawmakers are looking at keg-registration laws in order to keep better track of who buys what for whom, particularly when such kegs end up at parties heavily populated with minors. So far, 24 states and the District of Columbia have adopted keg registration laws of varying severity.

The Facts About Binge Drinking

- In 2001, 44% of U.S. college students engaged in binge drinking; this rate has not changed since 1993.

- 51% of the men drank five or more drinks in a row.

- 40% of the women drank four or more drinks in a row.

- Students more likely to binge drink are white, age 23 or younger, and are residents of a fraternity or sorority.

- 75.1% of fraternity residents and 62.4% of sorority residents report binge drinking.

- Binge drinkers in high school are three times more likely to binge in college.

- From 1993 to 2001, more students abstained from alcohol (16% to 19%), but more also frequently drank heavily (19.7% to 22.8%).

- Just as many freshmen (those under 21) as seniors binge drink.

- Frequent binge drinkers are eight times more likely than others to miss a class, fall behind in schoolwork, get hurt or injured, and damage property.

- 91% of women and 78% of the men who are frequent binge drinkers consider themselves to be moderate or light drinkers.

- 1,400 college students every year die from alcohol-related causes; 1,100 of these deaths involve drinking and driving.

Legislative Tools

"It is only a tool that might possibly reduce binge drinking and underage drinking," says Arizona Representative Ted Downing, who has introduced legislation requiring the state to put tracking numbers on every keg of beer sold.

"The way my legislation reads is that if you want to buy a keg, you have to show identification, fill out a form, leave a deposit, and detail where the keg is going to go and for what purpose" says Downing.

Other lawmakers believe that by making underage consumption and distribution more legally challenging, they can, at the very least, chip away at the roughly 33 percent of the nation's college students who are below the age of 21.

"It's worth a try," says Colorado Representative Angie Paccione, who has introduced legislation making it a class one misdemeanor to distribute alcohol to someone under the age of 21, with jail time of up to 18 months and fines topping out at $5,000.

"We want to give the Das [district attorneys] a tool that they can use for prosecuting and that the police can use in order to effect behavior changes," Paccione says, adding that problem college drinking is very often proceeded by problem high school drinking.

"I was a dean in a high school and have seen more than my share of kids who have had liquid lunches," she says. "So I know that this is a problem that begins very early."

Programs Work

And although a new look at both underage and binge drinking from the legislative perspective may be in order, Jeff Becker, president of the Beer Institute, says lawmakers should not lose sight of the progress that has already been made in reducing both high school and college drinking.

"The education and awareness programs have really worked, whether it is at the college or high school level; and I think lawmakers should take credit for any support they have given to those efforts and continue those programs," says Becker.

"Maybe these most recent deaths will serve as a wake-up call and get all of us to look once more at what works and what doesn't work," he adds. "But from the community, family and school level it is very clear that making kids aware of the dangers has also made them smarter. And I don't think we should stop doing that."

In Connecticut, Senator Biagio "Billy" Ciotto, a long-time advocate of programs that educate high school students on the harmful effects of both drinking and driving and binge drinking, says he remains convinced that lawmakers should concentrate on what he calls the "realistic goal of reduction" vs. the "impossible idea" of elimination.

"You are never going to get rid of this kind of drinking completely," Ciotto says. "But I have no doubt in my mind that you can reduce the abuse simply by staying with it, never giving up, always trying to let kids know, without lecturing them, about the harmful effects of alcohol abuse."

Help Those Who Want to Do the Right Thing

Ciotto's efforts have even won the support of the Connecticut Coalition to Stop Underage Drinking, which named him "Outstanding Legislator in Reducing Underage Drinking" in 2004.

"I think they and just about everyone else recognize that we have to work on the big majority of kids who will not abuse alcohol if they know the dangers, and just figure that there is always going to be a minority that will do what they want to do no matter what," he says.

Arizona's Downing agrees: "It would be very foolish for any state representative or senator to feel that you can propose a bill that will somehow magically get rid of the problems of binge drinking or underage drinking.

"You can't," says Downing. "And we have to admit that. All you can really do is nudge things in a certain direction, which is what so many of our laws do anyway. If people are going to behave in the wrong way no matter what, there is only so much we can do. But we can help those who want to do the right thing, or don't want to break any laws just to have a little fun. That is the group we need to appeal to."

The Government Should Not Censor Alcohol Advertising

Radley Balko

In this selection Radley Balko argues that research organizations sponsored by the anti-alcohol movement are promoting a neoprohibitionist agenda by calling for censorship of alcohol advertising along with other laws designed to reduce the availability of alcohol. He writes that policy makers adopt studies produced by these organizations without understanding that they are part of a well-organized effort to restrict the choices of all drinkers instead of holding individuals responsible for their own actions. Balko also describes the recommendations by several anti-alcohol groups to ban or unreasonably limit alcohol advertising on radio, television, and in print and their success in censoring statements on wine labels explaining the drink's health benefits. Keeping positive information secret affects the political climate, he writes, leading to popular support for bans on various types of alcohol advertising. In a free country, Balko concludes, the people should be able to choose what they drink without government interference. Radley Balko is a policy analyst for the libertarian research organization the Cato Institute and a columnist for FoxNews .com.

December 2003 mark[ed] the 70th anniversary of the Twenty-First Amendment, which repealed alcohol prohibition in the United States. The 13 years between the passage of the Eighteenth and Twenty-First Amendments saw the alcohol trade go underground, bringing with it all the ancillary crime that comes with a black market. Alcohol abuse in the United States went up, not down, and civil liberties and tax dollars were sacrificed to what amounted to a grand, failed experiment in state-enforced morality.

Radley Balko, "Back Door to Prohibition: The New War on Social Drinking," *Policy Analysis*, December 5, 2003. Copyright © 2003 Cato Institute. All rights reserved. Reproduced by permission.

One would think that, given the failure of Prohibition, Americans wouldn't need to worry about its return. That may not be the case. A well-funded movement of neoprohibitionists is afoot, with advocates in media, academia, and government.

The movement sponsors a variety of research organizations, which publish dozens of studies each year alleging the corruptive effects of alcohol. Those studies are taken at face value by well-intentioned policymakers at the local, state, and federal level. New laws are enacted that curb Americans' access to alcohol.

Some of those laws aim to make alcohol less available through taxation schemes, others through strict licensing or zoning requirements, still others by censoring alcohol advertisements. . . .

Taken together, the well-organized efforts of activists, law enforcement, and policymakers portend an approaching "backdoor prohibition"—an effort to curb what some of them call the "environment of alcoholism"—instead of holding individual drinkers responsible for their actions. Policymakers should be wary of attempts to restrict choice when it comes to alcohol. Such policies place the external costs attributable to a small number of alcohol abusers on the large percentage of people who consume alcohol responsibly. Those efforts didn't work when enacted as a wide-scale, federal prohibition, and they are also ineffective and counterproductive when implemented incrementally. . . .

Attempts to Ban Alcohol Advertising

The campaign against alcohol seeks to expand censorship precedents that have already been established for tobacco products. A September 2003 *Christian Science Monitor* editorial says: "Congress banned cigarette advertising from television and radio altogether, beginning in 1971. Doing the same with alcohol would be a good start." The editorial ran in response to a Federal Trade Commission report that an uncomfortable amount of alcohol advertising is reaching underage audiences. In response, the alcohol industry agreed to limit its advertising to media for which the underage audience is typically 30 percent or less of the total audience.

The *Christian Science Monitor* isn't alone.

- In a strategy conference hosted by the Educational Development Center in Boston [in 2003], a bevy of anti-alcohol advocacy organizations recommended banning all radio, television, and print alcohol advertising.

- The CASA [Columbia University's Center on Addiction and Substance Abuse] "Teen Tipplers" study [released Feb. 26, 2002,] ... was released just as the NBC television network was considering allowing liquor companies to run commercials during some of its programming. Rep. Frank Wolf (R-VA) and 12 other members of Congress sent a letter to NBC promising regulatory retaliation if the network went through with its plans. "We would hate to see your network become the object of a public backlash against network hard-liquor advertising or the reason that Congress steps in to protect the public interest and public airwaves by setting up a federal regulatory system for network advertising," the letter said.

- After a study by the Center for Alcohol Marketing to Youth criticized the alcohol industry for targeting its advertising at underage drinkers (including advertising on television programs that air during the school day and, in some cases, as late as 11 p.m. or midnight), Sens. Mike DeWine (R-OH) and Christopher Dodd (D-CT) issued a joint press release announcing their "intention to monitor underage drinking trends and the extent to which alcohol industry advertising is reaching underage youth." "We intend to hold advertisers accountable," Dodd said. "Our families and our children in Connecticut and Ohio and all across the nation deserve better."

- In their 1996 *Book Count*, former drug czar William J. Bennett, former White House aide John J. Dilulio Jr., and current drug czar John P. Walters have a section titled "Restricting Alcohol, Cutting Crime." In their proposal to limit the negative externalities [secondary consequences] of alcohol abuse, the authors advocate making "strong efforts to limit alcoholic beverage advertising." They write, "The alcohol industry seems perfectly well aware of the relationship among alcohol, disorder and crime—and in some infamous cases, has been quick to exploit it for commercial gain." Instead of calling for an outright ban on billboard advertisements the authors seek to accomplish the same end indirectly by enforcing limits on billboard advertising of alcohol and banning alcohol ads "from the *horizons* of schools, churches, and public housing centers."

Health Information Censored

In 1999 the Bureau of Alcohol, Tobacco and Firearms [BATF] approved a proposal from winemakers to include "directional" health statements on wine labels, which advised consumers to contact their personal physicians or consult government agencies to learn more about recent research indicating the health benefits of moderate alcohol consumption.

Two statements were allowed only after a litany of negative warnings about alcohol use and were hardly ringing endorsements. One said, "Alcoholic beverages have been used to enhance the enjoyment of meals by many societies throughout human history," and the other said, "Current evidence suggests that moderate drinking is associated with a lower risk for coronary heart disease in some individuals." Allowing the new labels made sense because at the time, despite recent research touting the health benefits of wine, polls showed that most Americans were still unaware of them.

But in 2003, after heavy lobbying from anti-alcohol groups, the BATF successor agency in charge of alcohol, the Federal Tax and Trade Bureau, effectively negated BATF's 1999 ruling, decreeing that directional health statements could not be included on wine labels without additional disclaimers about the negative effects of alcohol consumption. The Center for Science in the Public Interest hailed the ruling, writing in a press release, "Although a blanket ban on all health claims and health-related statements would have been preferable, we believe the regulations effectively shut the door to industry efforts to promote the healthfulness of drinking."

The Government Squelches Debate

A 2003 poll by the Institute of Social Research at the University of Michigan found that 80 percent of respondents thought the health drawbacks of alcohol consumption far outweighed the benefits, and 44 percent thought the government was doing too little to regulate alcohol. Another poll by the American Beverage Institute taken in 1998 found 55 percent of respondents agreeing that the spirits industry is a "harm" or "great harm" to society. Half thought the same of the beer industry.

By preventing the alcohol industry from communicating the health benefits of its products, anti-alcohol groups and government agencies ensure that public debate about alcohol and public health will be dominated by anti-alcohol groups and government agencies. Keeping the public ignorant of alcohol's health benefits obviously makes it easier to enact policies that restrict the public's access to alcohol. The point here is a very modest one: "Self-serving" statements from the liquor industry are *not* automatically false. And statements from "public health" activists are not automatically true.

Suppressing Positive Information

There's evidence that the strategy of suppressing positive information does affect the political climate. A December 2002 survey by the Alcohol Epidemiology Program at the University of Minnesota, for example, found that 70 percent of respondents favor outright bans on "youth-oriented" alcohol packaging, 67 percent favor banning liquor commercials on television, 62 percent favor banning "alcohol marketing with athletes," and 61 percent favor banning all billboard advertisements of alcohol. The billboard ban idea in particular has found resonance in cities across the country and has been the subject of several court battles. On its website, the Alcohol Epidemiology Program recommends that proponents of billboard bans cite poll statistics to get around objections from detractors. Not surprisingly, several cities have converted those recommendations and survey results into policy.

- In 1998 the city of Oakland, California, adopted an ordinance prohibiting alcohol advertising within three blocks of any recreation center, church, or day care facility. The ordinance left only 70 of the city's 1,450 billboards available for alcohol advertising.

- The city of San Diego passed a similar ordinance, removing over half of the city's billboard space from use by beer and alcohol industry firms.

- Baltimore has banned the advertisement of alcohol or tobacco in any "publicly visible location."

- Chicago adopted an ordinance based on Baltimore's model.

- Los Angeles; Washington, DC; Seattle; and Albuquerque are considering, but haven't yet adopted, the Baltimore model.

Just how those bans will hold up to First Amendment scrutiny isn't yet clear. The Baltimore ban was upheld by a federal appellate court in 1994. In *Anheuser-Busch v. Schmoke*, the Fourth Circuit Court of Appeals held that restrictions on commercial speech were allowable under the First Amendment so long as the restrictions were narrowly drawn to address a substantial government interest, as outlined in the landmark commercial speech case *Central Hudson Gas and Electric v. Public Service Commission*. The court held that the city of Baltimore's interest in minimizing the external effects of alcohol was substantial and that the restrictions banning certain substances from billboard ads were narrow enough to satisfy the First Amendment. The U.S. Supreme Court declined to hear an appeal from Anheuser-Busch.

Constitutional Limits on Censorship of Advertising

However, in the 1996 case *44 Liquormart, Inc. v. Rhode Island*, the Supreme Court overturned a Rhode Island law banning offsite advertising of alcohol prices. Rhode Island officials maintained that the ads would drive down the price of alcohol and that there was a compelling state interest in preventing increased consumption. Hence, the state conceded that the chief aim of the ad moratorium was not to address any "externality" related to alcohol abuse. Rather, the chief aim was to diminish the *lawful* consumption of alcohol.

The Supreme Court held that a state must meet a heavy burden in prohibiting commercial speech relating to a legal activity and that the state's interest in limiting alcohol consumption wasn't sufficient to justify an outright ban. In a concurring opinion, Justice Clarence Thomas went even further. Thomas wrote that Rhode Island's "asserted interest is to keep legal users of a product or service ignorant in order to manipulate their choices in the marketplace," and that in such cases "such an 'interest' is *per se* illegitimate and can no more justify regulation of 'commercial' speech than it can justify regulation of 'noncommercial' speech."

Most recently, in April 2003 the U.S. Court of Appeals for the Sixth Circuit struck down a Cleveland city ordinance that banned alcohol billboard advertisements in residential areas and limited them to a few designated districts within the city. However the courts come down on the constitutionality of bans on alcohol advertising, civil libertarians ought to be disturbed by the latest efforts to curb a *legal* industry's efforts to promote its product. The most prominent advocates of billboard bans and restrictions on alcohol advertising on TV and radio and at sporting events have made no secret of their intent to follow the example set by similar bans on tobacco products. Sandy Golden, a spokesperson for the Campaign for Alcohol-Free Kids, has said, "We're 10 to 15 years behind the tobacco people, and we want to close the gap."

Rhode Island's defense of its ban on alcohol advertising could not have been more clear. The aim of measures enacted to limit the scope and reach of alcohol advertising is, simply, to depress the consumption of alcohol. In a free society, politicians should not concern themselves with the diets of their constituents. At most, the surgeon general might issue a report to prove that orange juice improves health but that, say, chewing gum is detrimental to health. Ultimately, however, Americans ought to make up their own minds about what they eat and drink, without the social engineering schemes of politicians.

Alcohol Advertising to Young People Should Be Limited

David H. Jernigan

Young people in the United States are exposed to large amounts of alcohol advertising; however, people disagree about whether advertising influences their decision to drink. In this selection David H. Jernigan describes studies that show that exposure to alcohol advertisements does increase underage drinking. A major 2006 longitudinal study using a national sample of young people in the United States, demonstrated measurable increases in underage drinking in environments with more alcohol advertisements. Jernigan argues that this study disproves the alcohol industry's claim that its media campaigns do not have an impact on underage drinking. He also describes a Texas study showing that the use of music, stories, and humor in alcohol ads attract young drinkers and concludes that public health efforts to reduce underage drinking should include efforts to limit young people's exposure to alcohol advertisements. David Jernigan is the executive director of the Center on Alcohol Marketing and Youth and a research associate professor at Georgetown University. He has worked as an advisor to the World Health Organization and the World Bank on alcohol issues.

Alcohol use is the leading drug problem among America's youth. Every day, 7,000 young people younger than 16 years take their first drink. According to the National Institute on Alcohol Abuse and Alcoholism (Bethesda, Md.), incidence of onset of alcohol dependence peaks in the US population at age 18 years and trails off by age 25 years. The Centers for Disease Control and Prevention (Atlanta, Ga.) estimate that more than 4,000 persons younger than 21 years die annually as a result of excessive drinking. And the drinking that young people do is excessive: more than 90% of the alcohol consumed by young people aged 12 to 20 years is drunk when the drinker is having 5 or more drinks on a single occasion, usually defined as within 2 hours.

When it looked at underage drinking in the context of a 1999 report on self-regulation in the alcohol industry, the Federal Trade Commission concluded that, "While many factors may influence an underage person's drinking decisions, including among other things parents, peers and the media, there is reason to believe that advertising also plays a role." As [researcher Leslie B.] Snyder et al. have demonstrated . . . , these reasons are growing.

What is not in dispute is that young people in the United States see a lot of alcohol advertising. According to studies by the Center on Alcohol Marketing and Youth at Georgetown University (Washington, DC), in magazines in 2003, young people aged 12 to 20 years were exposed per capita to 48% more beer advertising, 20% more distilled spirits advertising, and 92% more advertising for "alcopops" (sweet, fizzy drinks such as Skyy Blue or Seagram's Smooth) than adults of the legal drinking age. Regression analysis [a statistical method to predict the average of random variables] of the relationship between adolescent audiences and alcohol ad placements in 35 major US magazines that included alcohol ads found, after controlling for a variety of other factors, that beer and distilled spirits advertisements appeared more frequently in magazines with audiences with higher adolescent readerships. From 1997 through 2001, there were 1.6 times more beer advertisements for each additional 1 million readers aged 12 to 19 years, but no association between beer advertisements and each additional 1 million readers aged 20 to 24 years. In the first 7 months of 2004—after the Beer Institute (Washington, DC) and the Distilled Spirits Council of the United States

(Washington, DC) changed their self-regulatory codes in September 2003 to reduce the maximum youth audience threshold for alcohol advertising from 50% to 30%—73 alcohol brands exposed more youth aged 12 to 20 years per capita to their magazine advertising than adults aged 21 years and older.

Youth Exposure to Alcohol Ads

On television from 2001 to 2003, 12- to 20-year-olds were more likely per capita than adults of the legal drinking age to have seen close to a quarter of the more than 750,000 alcohol product advertisements placed on broadcast and cable networks and local broadcast stations. Across those years, young people aged 12 to 20 years saw an average of 779 alcohol ads on television while the heaviest-watching 30% of that age group saw more than 1700 alcohol ads on television. In the first 10 months of 2004, at least 25 alcohol brands gained half their youth exposure from ads that young people aged 12 to 20 years were more likely to see per capita than adults.

On the radio, which is, after television, the second most popular medium for teenagers, an analysis of audiences for a sample of 51,883 commercials for the leading 25 alcohol brands in 104 markets in the summer of 2003 found that in 14 of the 15 largest markets, young people heard more alcohol product advertising per capita than adults aged 21 years and over. In 5 of the top 15 markets, they heard more alcohol advertising than adults aged 21 to 34 years, the group sometimes identified as the actual target for alcohol advertising.

Alcohol producers, like the tobacco companies in earlier years, have argued that alcohol advertising has no influence on alcohol consumption among young people. Although a number of cross-sectional studies in the United States and longitudinal studies from other countries suggested otherwise, the lack of longitudinal data on alcohol advertising and youth alcohol consumption in the United States has hampered the policy debate over whether or how young people should be protected from alcohol advertising.

Advertising's Influence

In 1998, the National Institute on Alcohol Abuse and Alcoholism, recognizing this deficit, funded several research groups to conduct these longitudinal studies. One group, starting with a sample of 2,250 seventh-graders in Los Angeles County public schools, and using a combination of exposure and recall variables [the amount of advertising that was seen and remembered], has found that an increase in viewing television programs containing alcohol commercials was associated 1 year later with a 44% excess risk of beer use, a 34% excess risk of wine or liquor use, and a 26% excess risk of engaging in 3-drink episodes. Another group followed 3,111 students in middle schools in South Dakota over 3 years and found that exposure to in-store beer displays predicted onset of drinking for non-drinkers after 2 years and that exposure to advertising in magazines and beer concession stands at sports or music events predicted greater frequency of drinking among drinkers after 2 years. This group found no significant predictive effect of exposure to television advertising for either drinkers or nondrinkers.

The work of Snyder et al. marks the first time that a national longitudinal sample of young people in the United States has been studied and the first time that self-reported exposure has been complemented by an objective measure of how much alcohol advertising is available in the media environment in which young people live. Their findings—that for underage drinkers, exposure to an additional alcohol ad was correlated with a 1% increase in drinking and that an additional dollar per capita spent on alcohol advertising in a local market was correlated with a 3% increase in underage alcohol consumption—calls into question the industry's argument that its roughly $1.8 billion in measured media expenditures per year have no impact on underage drinking. The fact that young people, regardless of drinking behavior at baseline, were more likely to drink more over time in environments with more alcohol advertising, even when controlling for alcohol sales in those environments, suggests that it is exposure to alcohol advertising that contributes to the drinking, rather than the reverse.

Snyder et al. do not delve into the question of how alcohol advertising influences young people, but another of the research groups funded by the National Institute on Alcohol Abuse and Alcoholism has. Findings from another longitudinal study, reported at the Research Society on Alcoholism (Austin, Tex.) meetings in June 2004, indicate that underage youth are drawn to elements of music, characters, story, and humor in alcohol advertising (as opposed, for example, to descriptions of product characteristics). Liking the ads was in turn correlated with the beliefs that positive outcomes from drinking were likely, that peers were likely to drink, and that peers were likely to approve of drinking. These beliefs appear to interact to produce greater intentions to drink and likelihood of drinking at later points in time.

Limiting Advertising Will Reduce Alcohol's Appeal

All these findings point to alcohol advertising as an important arena for interventions seeking to reduce underage drinking and its tragic consequences. Public health action on underage drinking rests on 2 key pillars: reducing the access of youth to alcohol and reducing the appeal of alcohol to young people. Policy changes, such as stricter enforcement of minimum age drinking laws; increases in alcohol prices through higher taxes or elimination of happy hours and other forms of discounting; and attention to the physical availability of alcohol, such as high concentrations of alcohol outlets near schools, have been suggested to reduce youth access to alcohol. The latter goal, reducing appeal, could be achieved, as the National Research Council (Washington, DC) and Institute of Medicine (Washington, DC) have recommended, through a national media campaign on underage drinking comparable with the existing paid media campaigns on tobacco and illegal drug use, as well as by limiting youth exposure to alcohol advertising.

The Center on Alcohol Marketing and Youth has found that through the simple act of reallocating television expenditures on alcohol advertising to programming with youth audiences of less than 15% (roughly the percentage of youth aged 12 to 20 years in the general population aged 12 years and above), alcohol companies could reduce their advertising expenditures by 8% with virtually no change in their ability to reach their often-stated target audience of 21- to 34-year-olds. This change would leave 79% of television programming available for alcohol advertising and would reduce youth exposure to alcohol advertising on television by 20%.

Federal surveys indicate that youth drinking stopped declining a decade ago [mid-1990s]. This led the National Research Council and Institute of Medicine to conclude that further progress in reducing this problem requires "significant new intervention." The research support for interventions on the "demand" side of the equation is growing. The work of Snyder et al. suggests that if alcohol companies were to reduce the number of alcohol ads young people see by adopting a 15% maximum threshold for youth audiences for alcohol advertising, they could make a substantial contribution to reducing underage drinking.

Stronger Laws Stop Hard-Core Drunk Drivers

Jeanne Mejeur

Drunk drivers with extremely high blood alcohol concentrations (BAC)—often more than twice the legal limit—are responsible for a large percentage of alcohol-related fatalities. In this selection Jeanne Mejeur explains the tragic impact of such drivers and discusses the two-tiered system of laws that some states have enacted, which prescribe higher penalties for very drunk drivers. She examines these penalties and concludes that stiffer sanctions have proved effective in reducing repeat offenses by extremely drunk drivers. Mejeur also writes about the importance of obtaining BAC measurements from suspected drunk drivers; in many states, the penalty for refusing a BAC test is much lower than the penalty for driving drunk. By increasing the penalties for refusing BAC tests, some states have succeeded in reducing the number of test refusals. Another effective tool in preventing very drunk drivers from repeating the offense, she writes, is the use of ignition interlocks, which require a driver to blow into a device that will prevent the car from starting if the driver has alcohol on his or her breath. Despite the progress made in reducing drunk driving deaths over the past thirty years, she argues, more can and must be done. Jeanne Mejeur writes for State Legislatures, *the journal of the National Conference of State Legislatures. She is also the conference's expert on drunk driving laws.*

All are sad stories; some are heartbreaking. Kris Mansfield survived his tour of duty in Iraq, only to be killed by a drunk driver less than four months after coming home to Colorado. The drunk driver's blood alcohol content (BAC) was an extremely high .217.

Seven-year-old Katie Flynn was the flower girl in her aunt's wedding and was riding home from the ceremony when their limousine was hit by a drunk driver going the wrong way on a Long Island parkway. Katie was killed instantly, along with the limo driver. Six members of the family were seriously injured. The drunk driver's BAC was .28.

These stories have more in common than a young life tragically cut short. The drivers in both instances were extremely drunk, about three times the legal limit. High BAC drivers are one of the most persistent and intractable facets of the drunk driving problem.

Extremely Drunk and Driving

Of the more than 42,000 traffic deaths in 2003, 40 percent were alcohol related. Twenty-two percent involved drivers with BAC levels in excess of .16. That's twice the legal limit of .08. It's also incredibly impaired.

"High BAC drivers are overrepresented in alcohol-related fatal crashes," says Anne McCartt, vice president for research at the Insurance Institute for Highway Safety. "For this reason, there's nothing misguided about deterrence programs targeting them."

At least 32 states have enacted high BAC laws, often called aggravated or extreme drunk driving. States with high BAC laws establish a two-tiered system of drunk driving offenses. The basic drunk driving limit is still set at .08, but a second, higher BAC level is established for drivers who are very drunk. States' high BAC thresholds range from .15 to .20.

Stronger Sanctions Work

Some states impose stiffer penalties for a high BAC offense, while others make it a separate offense, with separate penalties. At least 11 states considered bills to establish a high BAC threshold during the 2005 legislative session, but the only bill to pass was in Texas. The new law imposes higher fines and ignition interlocks for drivers with a BAC in excess of .15.

Are high BAC laws effective? The National Highway Traffic Safety Administration (NHTSA) says yes. In a study of Minnesota's laws, "Enhanced Sanctions for Higher BACs: Evaluation of Minnesota's High-BAC Law," published in 2004, NHTSA found that they worked. Minnesota's high BAC threshold is relatively high, at .20, but strong sanctions have made it effective. The study found that the high BAC law lowered recidivism and refuel rates among high BAC first-time offenders.

Get a BAC Test

It's hard to prosecute a drunk driver if you don't have a BAC test result. Juries want to know how drunk the driver was. For prosecutors, it's the single most important piece of evidence. It's a big problem, however, because nationwide, about a quarter of drivers refuse to be tested. In Louisiana, Massachusetts, Ohio and Texas, the refusal rate is more than 40 percent. In New Hampshire and Rhode Island, more than 80 percent of allegedly drunk drivers refuse.

In many states, the punishment for refusal is light—generally a license suspension. Compare that to the penalties for a conviction, which at a minimum include a suspended license, fines, jail time and probation. It's no wonder many drunk drivers refuse the test.

So at least 15 states have made it harder to refuse. They've adopted criminal penalties for refusal that include hefty fines and jail time. In Alaska, Minnesota and Vermont, the penalties for refusing to be tested are the same as for being convicted of drunk driving. Advocates believe that faced with harsher penalties for refusing, more drunk drivers will take a BAC test, hoping that they'll pass.

Getting drivers to take BAC tests may have broader benefits. "Reducing test refusals increases the effectiveness of the criminal system so offenders can't avoid penalties. It can also identify problem drinkers, and help them get some help," according to Dr. Thomas Zwicker, senior research associate with the Preusser Research Group in Connecticut.

Require Ignition Interlocks

Many high BAC drivers are repeat offenders. So a number of states now require them to have an ignition interlock installed on their vehicle.

The device is similar to the Breathalyzers police use. The driver blows into the ignition interlock before starting the car. If the device detects alcohol in the person's breath, the car won't start. Some devices require frequent retesting while the car is running, to ensure that the driver isn't drinking while driving.

Judges typically have the discretion to order the installation of ignition interlocks as part of sentencing for convicted drunk drivers. In states where use of ignition interlocks is mandatory, they are generally required only for repeat offenders, as a condition of probation, or for restoration of limited driving privileges.

New Mexico's Law Is Successful

New Mexico passed a law in 2005 making it the first state in the nation to mandate ignition interlocks for all convicted drunk drivers, including first time offenders. "It's a great use of new technology and behavior modification wrapped up into one," says Senator Kent Cravens, who co-sponsored the law with Representative Ken Martinez. Senator Cravens knows first-hand the pain caused by drunk drivers. His sister-in-law and three nieces were killed and his brother severely injured by a drunk driver in a tragic Christmas Eve accident in 1992.

The New Mexico law requires all convicted drunk drivers to apply for an "Ignition Interlock License" permitting them to drive legally on a revoked license once they have an ignition interlock installed. Drivers who don't apply because they don't have a vehicle or claim they won't drive can be sentenced to house arrest.

Approximately 6,000 interlocks have been installed in New Mexico so far. According to the New Mexico Department of Transportation, offenders who have an ignition interlock installed on their vehicle have 75 percent fewer drunk driving arrests than those without interlocks.

Treat Substance Abuse

Drivers with drinking or drug addictions are more likely to become repeat offenders or to drive when extremely impaired. Addressing underlying substance abuse problems is critical in stopping the cycle, experts say.

More than half the states require convicted drunk drivers to attend education programs on alcohol and drug abuse. And a growing number of states are requiring substance abuse education even for first time offenders.

But for some, education is not enough. Judges in almost all states have the discretion to require offenders to undergo substance abuse treatment as part of their sentences. Many states require education and treatment for limited restoration of driving privileges or as a condition of probation. Getting convicted impaired drivers into treatment for drinking or drug problems helps to curb repeated offenses.

High Death Toll

States have made great progress over the last three decades in reducing drunk driving fatalities. In the past, alcohol was involved in more than half of traffic fatalities. Now it's down to about 40 percent. But there's still a long way to go in reducing drunk driving deaths.

Like those about Kris Mansfield and Katie Flynn, there are thousands of tragic drunk driving stories each year. In 2004, 16,694 deaths were caused by impaired drivers. That's about 320 people a week, roughly the equivalent of a weekly plane crash killing everyone on board. If that were happening, no one would fly and the public would clamor for action. Because drunk driving deaths generally involve only one or two victims at a time and they're spread all over the country, the death toll isn't as obvious as a weekly plane crash. But the number of deaths is the same.

And each story is personal. Glynn R. Birch, national president of MADD, lost his 21-month-old son to a drunk driver. "MADD continues to remind the country that drunk driving should not be tolerated, by placing the faces of loved ones on the cold, hard statistics that litter our roadways," says Birch. Considering the thousands of families affected every year, it's time for a renewed commitment to get hardcore drunk drivers off the roads for good.

Stronger Laws Against Drunk Driving Violate Personal Freedoms

Richard Berman

In this selection Richard Berman argues that the hidden agenda of anti-alcohol organizations such as Mothers Against Drunk Driving (MADD) is to institute de facto prohibition. He describes several examples of small steps proposed by what he calls neoprohibitionists, including mandating that all cars have ignition interlocks that require a driver to blow into a device that will prevent the car from starting if his or her blood alcohol concentration is too high, making it illegal for anyone convicted of driving under the influence to buy alcohol for five years, increasing alcohol taxes and roadblocks, and lowering the legal limit for blood alcohol concentration for suspected drunk drivers. Berman writes that the alcohol industry has undertaken effective innovations to combat drunk driving, such as designated driver programs, that antialcohol activists have opposed. He argues that the hidden agenda of neoprohibitionists is ultimately to ban all consumption of alcohol. Richard Berman is executive director of the Center for Consumer Freedom, which represents the interests of the food, alcohol, and tobacco industries. He is also president of Berman and Company, a research, communications, advertising, and government affairs firm.

The slow, silent march to alcohol prohibition continues apace.

In March [2004], Mothers Against Drunk Driving called for a "mandatory provision in every separation agreement and

Richard Berman, "Recalling Prohibition Best Way for Operators to Halt Progress of Anti-alcohol Campaigns (Berman on Offense)," *Nation's Restaurant News*, vol. 38, May 24, 2004, p. 38. Copyright © 2004 Nation's Restaurant News. Reprinted by permission of the publisher.

divorce decree that prohibits either parent from drinking and driving . . . with children under the age of 16 in the vehicle." Any drinking before driving, MADD insisted, should result in "termination of parental rights." Have one glass of wine with dinner, and the kids are gone.

MADD's assault on divorced parents, as with all its efforts in recent years, isn't about traffic safety; it's about marginalizing and eventually criminalizing any drinking before driving—one subgroup at a time.

For example, it advocates a nationwide arrest threshold of 0.05-percent blood alcohol concentration, or BAC, for repeat offenders with kids in the car. MADD literally is seeking to redefine the term "drunk" for certain populations—yet another incremental step toward de facto prohibition.

Small Steps Toward Prohibition

It's no coincidence that MADD's 0.05-percent proposal is identical to a recently passed Utah law written by George Van Komen, who opposes all alcohol consumption. Van Komen leads an organization formerly called both the "Anti-Saloon League" and the "National Temperance League." Other examples of neoprohibitionist "small steps" from 2004 alone include the following:

- Legislators in New Mexico, New York and Oklahoma introduced legislation to mandate ignition interlocks in every car. New York State Assemblyman Felix Ortiz even admitted that with his breathalyzer bill, "We are targeting responsible adults." While none of those proposals will become law [in 2004], they are a first step in an attempt to desensitize the public to an outrageously neoprohibitionist plan.

- The White House's Office of National Drug Control Policy linked alcohol with drug use for the first time in its five-year media campaign. It already has aired the alcohol-drugs connection in a 30-second Super Bowl spot and in an "open letter" published in almost 300 newspapers.

- The other Bush administration—that of Florida governor Jeb Bush—announced that his state "is prepared to reduce underage drinking by serving as a pilot" for a plan that includes increased alcohol taxes and roadblocks.

- Bill Richardson, the governor of New Mexico . . . expressed interest in a bill to ban anyone convicted of a DUI, or driving under the influence, from buying liquor for five years.

- Adopting the slogan "If you drink and drive, you lose your ride," the Los Angeles City Council now is considering the Giuliani-esque tactic of seizing and auctioning off suspected drunk drivers' cars—before they've been to court and convicted of the crime.

- The National Institute on Alcohol Abuse and Alcoholism lowered its threshold in defining "drunk." Now "binge drinking" means reaching .08 percent BAC. A person is engaging in "risky drinking" if he reaches just .05 percent BAC. So if you serve a customer as few as two drinks over a meal, you're facilitating "risky" behavior.

Collective Impact of Minor Compromises

Anti-alcohol activists, in order to achieve their long-term goal of drastically reducing consumption across the board, have adopted a game plan that spans decades. Industry executives, in contrast, serve for relatively brief periods. When executives enter an environment where .08 percent BAC is the law of the land and "Don't Drink & Drive" is the accepted mantra, those standards become the starting point for the next round of negotiations—and the activists always demand more. Minor

155

compromises by business seem reasonable in an attempt to be "responsible." But collectively, those concessions add up to significant erosions over time.

There's an old wives' tale that says if you put a frog in water and gradually raise the temperature, it won't detect the incremental increases and eventually will be scalded to death.

Neoprohibitionists view industry executives—and the public—as that frog. If they restrain themselves and only turn up the heat gradually, no one will notice.

We no longer can afford to fight each small battle on the field chosen by neoprohibitionists. Industry can win over public opinion with a "future shock" campaign. Let Americans know what the world will look like in 10 years if MADD achieves its ultimate objectives.

Alcohol Industry's Anti-Drunk-Driving Innovations

Almost all Americans share an instinctive aversion to outright prohibition, and we can win back the moral high ground if we successfully broadcast the neoprohibitionists' radical agenda.

Our side enjoys a huge—although largely untapped—communications advantage. Restaurants and off-premises licensees have an unparalleled capacity to speak to consumers at the point of purchase. Why not use that power to send out a message?

When drunk driving emerged in the social consciousness in the 1980s, adult-beverage suppliers and retailers were at the forefront of the struggle to address it. The industry sought to prevent occasional product abuse by otherwise-responsible adults through designated-driver programs, taxi rides and public education campaigns. Restaurants and taverns incorporated proof-of-age and server-education programs into their employee training.

Activists Oppose Designated Driver Programs

Today those industry programs that activists once encouraged and endorsed are dismissed by the very same groups as "ineffective" and having "minimal or no impact." Neoprohibitionists, in their zeal to reduce per-capita consumption, even have attacked the concept of a designated driver.

"The presence of a designated driver encourages the nondrivers to drink more than they would otherwise," one widely circulated anti-alcohol report whines. MADD has attacked a bus service that brings people to and from bars because it facilitates drinking. And the group's president recently wrote: "The thought that [driving] can be successfully combined with alcohol on the part of the driver or even the passengers defies any logic I can imagine."

Read that again: "even the passengers."

The Effect of Fetal Alcohol Exposure on the Developing Brain

National Institute on Alcohol Abuse and Alcoholism

In this selection the National Institute on Alcohol Abuse and Alcoholism (NIAAA) updates its earlier bulletin on fetal alcohol syndrome (FAS) with new information on how frequently neurobehavioral problems result from fetal alcohol exposure and the nature of those problems. In the past, fetal alcohol exposure was thought to impair development in general; however, recent studies show that certain brain functions are impacted while others go unharmed. The article explains that using modern imaging techniques, doctors can see whether the brain of a fetus has been damaged by exposure to alcohol. Experiments suggest that substances such as antioxidants may repair some of the damage, and the NIAAA recommends that further research in that area be carried out. The NIAAA is part of the U.S. Department of Health and Human Services' Public Health Service and the National Institutes of Health.

Nearly 30 years ago, scientists first coined the term "fetal alcohol syndrome" (FAS) to describe a pattern of birth defects found in children of mothers who consumed alcohol during pregnancy. Today, FAS remains the leading known preventable cause of mental retardation. Behavioral and neurological problems associated with prenatal alcohol exposure may lead to poor academic performance as well as legal and employment difficulties in adolescence and adulthood. Despite attempts to increase public awareness of the risks involved, increasing numbers of women are drinking during pregnancy.

National Institute on Alcohol Abuse and Alcoholism, "Alcohol Alert," no. 50, NIAAA, December 2000, http://pubs.niaaa.nih.gov/publications/aa50.htm.

This bulletin updates *Alcohol Alert* No. 13 with new data on the prevalence and nature of the neurobehavioral problems associated with alcohol use during pregnancy, explores potential mechanisms underlying alcohol-induced damage to the developing brain, and discusses prevention research.

FAS is defined by four criteria: maternal drinking during pregnancy; a characteristic pattern of facial abnormalities; growth retardation; and brain damage, which often is manifested by intellectual difficulties or behavioral problems. When signs of brain damage appear following fetal alcohol exposure in the absence of other indications of FAS, the condition is termed "alcohol-related neurodevelopmental disorder" (ARND).

Investigators have used both passive and active methods to determine the overall incidence of FAS and ARND. The passive approach uses data collected from existing medical records, which are often based on information recorded at birth. However, the criteria required for these diagnoses may not be apparent at birth and often develop gradually from infancy through the first few years of grade school. In the active approach, investigators use a defined set of diagnostic criteria to screen all members of a selected population for FAS and other alcohol-related problems. Although both strategies have limitations, active ascertainment provides more accurate prevalence data for the study population, especially if children are examined at elementary school age. For example, a comprehensive survey of 992 first-grade students in 12 of the 13 elementary schools in a South African community revealed an FAS incidence of more than 40 FAS cases per 1,000 births among children ages 5 to 9. In the United States, a preliminary active ascertainment of FAS in a single county in Washington State yielded a minimum estimate of 3.1 per 1,000 first-grade students. By comparison, passive estimates of FAS rates range from 0.33 to 3 infants per 1,000 births.

Specific Cognitive and Behavioral Impairments

The broad range of cognitive and behavioral disabilities associated with prenatal alcohol exposure was attributed by many researchers to a generalized impairment of mental functioning. However, recent studies on FAS and ARND reveal that specific neurobehavioral functions are consistently impaired, whereas others are spared. Thus, the outlook for persons diagnosed with FAS or ARND should not be considered hopeless. Some specific neurobehavioral impairments associated with prenatal alcohol exposure are discussed below.

Verbal Learning. Children prenatally exposed to alcohol exhibit a variety of problems with language and memory. For example, [S.N.] Mattson and colleagues found that children with FAS ages 5 to 16 learned fewer words compared with a group of children of comparable mental age who did not have FAS. However, both groups demonstrated equal ability to recall information learned previously. These findings indicate that FAS-related learning problems occur during the initial stages of memory formation (i.e., encoding). Once encoded, verbal information can be retained and recalled, subject to normal rates of forgetting. Clinically, this pattern helps distinguish FAS from Down's syndrome, in which learning and recall are equally impaired.

Visual-Spatial Learning. Children of mothers who drank heavily during pregnancy perform poorly on tasks that involve learning spatial relationships among objects. In one experiment, groups of children with and without FAS were equal in their ability to recall common, small household and schoolroom objects (e.g., a paper clip or spoon) that had been placed within sight on a table and then removed. However, children with FAS had greater difficulty subsequently restoring the objects to their original positions on the table.

Attention. Attention problems have been considered a hallmark of prenatal alcohol exposure. Consequently, FAS is often incorrectly diagnosed as attention deficit hyperactivity disorder (ADHD) and treated inappropriately. [C.D.] Coles and colleagues found that children with ADHD exhibited difficulty focusing and sustaining attention over time. In contrast, children who were exposed to alcohol prenatally were able to focus and maintain attention, but displayed difficulty in *shifting* attention from one task to another (i.e., set shifting).

Reaction Time. Individual differences in intelligence are based in part on how quickly the brain processes information. Prenatal alcohol exposure has been associated with slower, less efficient information processing in school-age children. Jacobson and colleagues found similar problems in children as young as 6 1/2 months. These researchers recorded the eye movements of infants reacting to the appearance, movement, and disappearance of a repeating sequence of geometric designs and colors on a video screen. Maternal drinking during pregnancy was related to longer reaction times among the children, suggesting slower, less efficient information processing.

Executive Functions. Important deficits in FAS involve executive functions (i.e., activities that require abstract thinking, such as planning and organizing). For example, problems with set shifting are common, as noted earlier. Children prenatally exposed to alcohol respond poorly when asked to switch from naming animals to naming types of furniture, and then back to naming animals. They also have difficulty abandoning demonstrably ineffective strategies when approaching problem-solving tasks, a type of behavioral inflexibility referred to as perseveration. Perseveration and impaired set shifting are consistent with distractibility and impulsivity, factors that at least theoretically might contribute to attention and learning problems.

Effects on Brain Structure

The behavioral and cognitive impairments associated with FAS reflect underlying structural or functional changes in the brain. Techniques for viewing the living brain, such as magnetic resonance imaging (MRI), reveal reduced overall brain size in persons with FAS and disproportionate reductions in the size of specific brain structures.

One such area is the deep-brain structure called the basal ganglia. Damage to the basal ganglia impairs spatial memory and set shifting in animals and various cognitive processes in humans. Another common finding is reduced size of the cerebellum, a structure involved in balance, gait, coordination, and cognition. Finally, prenatal alcohol exposure is the major cause of impaired development or complete absence of the corpus callosum, a band of nerve fibers that forms the major communication link between the right and left halves of the brain. Approximately 7 percent of children with FAS may lack a corpus callosum, an incidence rate 20 times higher than that in the general population.

The mechanisms that underlie alcohol-induced fetal brain damage have been studied in experimental animals and in nerve cells (i.e., neurons) grown in culture. Within the fetus, embryonic cells destined to become brain neurons grow in number, move to their ultimate locations, and mature into a wide variety of functionally distinct neuronal cell types, eventually forming connections with other brain cells in a predetermined pattern. Alcohol metabolism is associated with increased susceptibility to cell damage caused by potentially harmful substances called free radicals. Free radical damage can kill sensitive populations of brain cells at critical times of development in the first trimester of pregnancy. Other animal experiments suggest that the third trimester may also represent a particularly sensitive period for brain cell damage associated with FAS.

Alcohol or its metabolic breakdown products can also interfere with brain development by altering the production or function of natural regulatory substances that help promote the orderly growth and differentiation of neurons. Research using animals or cell cultures show that many of alcohol's adverse effects on brain cells can be prevented by treatments aimed at restoring the balance of regulatory substances upset by alcohol. Promising results have also been obtained in similar experiments by administering substances (i.e., antioxidants) that help protect cells against free radical-induced cell damage. This is only one of several potential mechanisms that may contribute to alcohol-related fetal injury. Further research is needed to determine if such an approach might prove both effective and safe in humans during pregnancy.

Effect of Maternal Drinking Levels

The minimum quantity of alcohol required to produce adverse fetal consequences is unknown. Clinically significant deficits are not common in children whose mothers drank less than approximately five drinks per occasion once per week. However, vulnerability to a given alcohol level during pregnancy varies markedly from person to person, possibly reflecting genetic factors, nutritional status, environmental factors, co-occurring diseases, and maternal age. FAS and ARND could be completely eliminated if pregnant women did not consume alcohol. Therefore, recent FAS prevention research has focused on finding and treating women who drink during pregnancy.

Pregnant women who are consuming alcohol but are not "problem" drinkers may decrease their drinking level following such an assessment without subsequent treatment. An overall decline in alcohol consumption has also been noted among pregnant women following a brief intervention, which can be conducted by a primary care provider. Such sessions may include a discussion of the risks of maternal drinking and suggested alternatives to alcohol use. Pregnant women with higher drinking levels may benefit from a 1-hour motivational interview focusing on the health of the unborn child. Women who are alcohol dependent require intensive alcoholism treatment.

The Health Benefits and Risks of Alcohol

The Nutrition Source, Dept. of Nutrition, Harvard School of Public Health

Alcohol is both a tonic and a poison. In the following article the Harvard School of Public Health summarizes and analyzes recent research on the risks and benefits of both moderate and excessive use of alcohol. The authors provide a definition of "moderate" drinking, a term often used loosely, and describe recent research on the cardiovascular benefits of moderate drinking. The authors conclude that alcohol almost certainly reduces the risk of heart disease. Additional benefits of alcohol include reduced risk of gallstones and type 2 diabetes, as well as improved digestion and relaxation, the authors note. The article also discusses the risks of overuse of alcohol, including violence, automobile accidents, liver and heart disease, and some cancers. In addition, the article explains that genetics play a role both in alcoholism and in the effect alcohol will have on an individual's health. The mission of the Harvard School of Public Health is to advance public health through education and communication.

Throughout the 10,000 or so years that humans have been drinking fermented beverages, they've also been arguing about their merits and demerits. The debate still simmers today, with a lively back-and-forth over whether alcohol is good for you or bad for you.

It's safe to say that alcohol is both a tonic and a poison. The difference lies mostly in the dose. Moderate drinking seems to be good for the heart and circulatory system, and probably protects against type 2 diabetes and gallstones. Heavy drinking is a major cause of preventable death in most coun-

The Nutrition Source, Dept. of Nutrition, Harvard School of Public Health, "Alcohol," www.hsph.harvard.edu/nutritionsource/alcohol.html, 2006. © 2006 President and Fellows of Harvard College. Reproduced by permission.

tries. In the U.S., alcohol is implicated in about half of fatal traffic accidents.[1] Heavy drinking can damage the liver and heart, harm an unborn child, increase the chances of developing breast and some other cancers, contribute to depression and violence, and interfere with relationships.

Alcohol's two-faced nature shouldn't come as a surprise. The active ingredient in alcoholic beverages, a simple molecule called ethanol, affects the body in many different ways. It directly influences the stomach, brain, heart, gallbladder, and liver. It affects levels of lipids (cholesterol and triglycerides) and insulin in the blood, as well as inflammation and coagulation. It also alters mood, concentration, and coordination.

What's "Moderate"? What's "a Drink"?

Loose use of terms has fueled some of the ongoing debate about alcohol's impact on health. In some studies, the term "moderate drinking" refers to less than one drink per day, while in others it means three or four drinks per day. Exactly what constitutes "a drink" is also fairly fluid. In fact, even among alcohol researchers, there's no universally accepted standard drink definition.[2] In the U.S., one drink is usually considered to be 12 ounces of beer, 5 ounces of wine, or 1 [frac12] ounces of spirits (hard liquor such as gin or whiskey).[3] Each delivers about 12 to 14 grams of alcohol.

The definition of moderate drinking is something of a balancing act. Moderate drinking sits at the point at which the health benefits of alcohol clearly outweigh the risks. The latest consensus places this point at no more than one to two drinks per day for men, and no more than one drink per day for women. This is the definition used by the U.S. Department of Agriculture and the Dietary Guidelines for Americans, and is widely used in the U.S.

Alcohol and Heart Disease

More than 100 prospective studies show an inverse association between moderate drinking and risk of heart attack, ischemic (clot-caused) stroke, peripheral vascular disease, sudden cardiac death, and death from all cardiovascular causes.[4] The effect is fairly consistent, corresponding to a 25–40% reduction in risk. . . . The connection between moderate drinking and lower risk of cardiovascular disease has been observed in men and women. It applies to people who do not apparently have heart disease. It also applies to those at high risk for having a heart attack or stroke or dying of cardiovascular disease—people with type 2 diabetes[5] and those with high blood pressure, angina (chest pain), a prior heart attack, or other forms of cardiovascular disease.[5-8]

The idea that moderate drinking protects against cardiovascular disease is biologically and scientifically plausible. Moderate amounts of alcohol raise levels of high-density lipoprotein (HDL, or "good" cholesterol),[6] and higher HDL levels are associated with greater protection against heart disease. Moderate alcohol consumption has also been linked with beneficial changes in a variety of factors that influence blood clotting, such as tissue type plasminogen activator, fibrinogen, clotting factor VII, and von Willebrand factor. Such changes would tend to prevent the formation of small blood clots that can block arteries in the heart, neck, and brain, the ultimate cause of many heart attacks and the most common kind of stroke.

Alcohol Probably Reduces Risk

People who drink in moderation are different from nondrinkers or heavy drinkers in ways that could influence health and disease. Part of a national 1985 health interview survey showed that moderate drinkers were more likely than nondrinkers or heavy drinkers to be at a healthy weight, to get 7–8 hours of sleep a night, and to exercise regularly[7]. Researchers have statistically accounted for such confounders, and they do not come close to accounting for the relationship between alcohol and heart disease. This, plus the clearly beneficial effects of alcohol on cardiovascular risk factors, makes a compelling case that alcohol itself, when used in moderation, reduces the risk of cardiovascular disease.

The most definitive way to investigate the effect of alcohol on cardiovascular disease would be with a large trial in which some volunteers were randomly assigned to have one or more alcoholic drinks a day and others had drinks that looked, tasted, and smelled like alcohol but were actually alcohol-free. Such a trial will probably never be done. Nevertheless, the connection between moderate drinking and cardiovascular disease almost certainly represents a cause-and-effect relationship.

Additional Benefits of Alcohol

The benefits of moderate drinking aren't limited to the heart. In both the Nurses' Health Study and the Health Professionals Follow-up Study, gallstones and type 2 diabetes were less likely to occur in moderate drinkers than in nondrinkers.[9-11]

The social and psychological benefits of alcohol can't be ignored. A drink before a meal can improve digestion or offer a soothing respite at the end of a stressful day; the occasional drink with friends can be a social tonic. These physical and psychic effects may contribute to health and wellbeing.

The Risks of Alcohol

If all drinkers limited themselves to a single drink a day, we probably wouldn't need as many cardiologists, liver specialists, mental health professionals, and substance abuse counselors. But not everyone who likes to drink alcohol stops at just one. While most people drink in moderation, some don't. Problem drinking affects not just the drinkers themselves, but may touch their families, friends, and communities. According to the National Institute on Alcohol Abuse and Alcoholism:[1]

- 14 million Americans meet standard criteria for alcohol abuse or alcoholism

- Alcohol plays a role in 1 in 4 cases of violent crime

- More than 16,000 people die each year in automobile accidents in which alcohol was involved

- Alcohol abuse costs more than $180 billion dollars a year

On the personal level, heavy drinking can take a toll on the body. It can cause inflammation of the liver (alcoholic hepatitis) and lead to scarring of the liver (cirrhosis), a potentially fatal disease. Heavy drinking can increase blood pressure and damage heart muscle (cardiomyopathy). It has also been linked with several cancers, particularly those of the mouth, throat, esophagus, colon, and breast.

Even moderate drinking carries some risks. Alcohol can disrupt sleep. Its ability to cloud judgment is legendary. Alcohol interacts in potentially dangerous ways with a variety of medications, including acetaminophen, antidepressants, anticonvulsants, painkillers, and sedatives. It is also addictive, especially for people with a family history of alcoholism.

Alcohol and Breast Cancer

Among women in the Nurses' Health Study, two or more drinks a day increased the chances of developing breast cancer by 20%–25%.[12,13] This doesn't mean that 20% to 25% of women who have two drinks a day will get breast cancer. Instead, it is the difference between about 12 of every 100 women developing breast cancer during their lifetimes—the current average risk in the US—and 14 to 15 of every 100 women developing the disease. This modest increase would translate to significantly more women with breast cancer each year. Adequate daily intake of folic acid, at least 600 milligrams a day, can mitigate this increased risk.

Studies of alcohol consumption and cardiovascular disease

Participants	Duration	Association with moderate consumption*
Kaiser Permanente cohort: 123,840 men and women aged 30+	10 years	40% reduction in fatal myocardial infarction, 20% reduction in cardiovascular mortality; 80% increase in fatal hemorrhagic stroke (23)
Nurses' Health Study: 85,709 female nurses aged 34–59	12 years	17% lower risk of all-cause mortality; (24) an earlier report showed a 40% reduction in risk of CHD and 70% reduction in risk of ischemic stroke (25)
Physicians' Health Study: 22,071 male physicians aged 40–84	11 years	30–35% reduced risk of angina and myocardial infarction, 20–30% reduced risk of cardio-vascular death (7, 26)
American Cancer Society cohort: 489,626 men and women aged 30–104	9 years	30–40% reduced risk of cardiovascular death (27)
Eastern France cohort: 34,014 men and women	10–15 years	25–30% reduced risk of cardiovascular death (28)
Health Professionals Follow-up Study: 38,077 male health professionals aged 40–75	12 years	35% reduced risk of myocardial infarction (20)

*compared with non-drinkers

SOURCE: Harvard School of Public Health.

The Vitamin-Alcohol-Cancer Connection

What is the connection between alcohol, folic acid, and breast cancer? Folic acid, the B vitamin that helps guide the development of an embryo's spinal cord has equally important jobs later in life. It helps the body get rid of homecysteine. This byproduct of protein metabolism appears to be involved with the development of atherosclerosis, the gradual accumulation of cholesterol-filled patches in artery walls that often precedes heart attacks and strokes. Folic acid also helps build DNA and so is involved with accurate cell division.

Alcohol blocks the absorption of folic acid and inactivates folic acid in the blood and tissues. It's possible that this interaction may be how alcohol consumption increased the risk of breast, colon, and other cancers.

Getting extra folic acid may cancel out this alcohol-related increase. In the Nurses' Health Study, for example, among women who consumed one alcoholic drink a day or more, those who had the highest levels of B vitamin in their blood were 90% less likely to develop breast cancer than those who had the lowest levels of B vitamin.[15] An earlier study suggests that getting 600 micrograms a day of folic acid could counteract the effect of moderate alcohol consumption on breast cancer risk.[16]

Similarly, an excess risk of colon cancer seen with the consumption of more than two drinks per day appears to be largely eliminated by adequate intake of folic acid.[17]

Based on this and other research, women and men who drink alcohol regularly should be sure to get an adequate intake of folic acid—at least 600 micrograms a day. This can be obtained through a healthy diet that is rich in fruits, vegetables, dry beans, and whole grains. Taking a multivitamin supplement (most contain 400 micrograms of folic acid) is also a good idea as a nutritional safety net.

Genes Play a Role

Twin, family, and adoption studies have firmly established that genetics plays an important role in determining an individual's preferences for alcohol and his or her likelihood for developing alcoholism. Alcoholism doesn't follow the simple rules of inheritance set out by [nineteenth-century genetics researcher] Gregor Mendel. Instead, it is influenced by several genes that interact with each other and with environmental factors.[1]

There is also some evidence that genes influence how alcohol affects the cardiovascular system. An enzyme called alcohol dehydrogenase helps metabolize alcohol. One variant of this enzyme, called alcohol dehydrogenase type 3 (ADH3), comes in two "flavors." One quickly breaks down alcohol, the other does it more slowly. Moderate drinkers who have two copies of the gene for the slow-acting enzyme are at much lower risk for cardiovascular disease than moderate drinkers who have two genes for the fast-acting enzyme.[14] Those with one gene for the slow-acting enzyme and one for the faster enzyme fall in between. It's possible that the fast-acting enzyme breaks down alcohol before it can have a beneficial effect on HDL and clotting factors.

Interestingly, these differences in the ADH3 gene do not influence the risk of heart disease among people who don't drink alcohol. This adds strong indirect evidence that alcohol itself reduces heart disease risk.

Shifting Benefits and Risks

The benefits and risks of moderate drinking change over a lifetime. In general, risks exceed benefits until middle age, when cardiovascular disease begins to account for increasingly large share of the burden of disease and death.

- For a pregnant woman and her unborn child, a recovering alcoholic, a person with liver disease, and people-taking one or more medications that interact with alcohol, moderate drinking offers little benefit and potential risks.

- For a 30-year-old man, the increased risk of alcohol-related accidents outweighs the possible heart-related benefits of moderate alcohol consumption.

- For a 60-year-old man, a drink a day may offer protection against heart disease that is likely to outweigh potential harm (assuming he isn't prone to alcoholism).

- For a 60-year-old woman, the benefit/risk calculations are trickier. More than ten times as many women die each year from heart disease than breast cancer—more than 500,000 women a year from cardiovascular disease compared with 41,000 a year from breast cancer. However, studies show that women are far more afraid of developing breast cancer than heart disease, something that must be factored into the equation.

Balancing Act

Given the complexity of alcohol's effects on the body and the complexity of the people who drink it, blanket recommendations about alcohol are out of the question. Because each of us has unique personal and family histories, alcohol offers each person a different spectrum of benefits and risks. Whether or not to drink alcohol, especially for "medicinal purposes," requires careful balancing of these benefits and risks. Your health-care provider should be able to help you do this.

Your overall health and risks for alcohol-associated conditions should factor into the equation. If you are thin, physically active, don't smoke, eat a healthy diet, and have no family history of heart disease, drinking alcohol won't add much to decreasing your risk of CVD [cardiovascular disease].

If you don't drink, there's no need to start. You can get similar benefits with exercise (beginning to exercise if you don't already or boosting the intensity and duration of your activity) or healthier eating. If you are a man with no history of alcoholism who is at moderate to high risk for heart disease, a daily alcoholic drink could reduce that risk. Moderate drinking might be especially beneficial if you have low HDL that just won't budge upward with diet and exercise. If you are a woman with no history of alcoholism who is at moderate to high risk for heart disease, the possible benefits of a daily drink must be balanced against the small increase in risk of breast cancer.

If you already drink alcohol or plan to begin, keep it moderate—no more than two drinks a day for men or one drink a day for women. And make sure you get plenty of folic acid, at least 600 micrograms a day.

Is Wine Fine, or Beer Better?

Almost 200 years ago, an Irish doctor noted that chest pain (angina) was far less common in France than in Ireland. He attributed the difference to "the French habits and mode of living."[17]

The comparatively low rate of heart disease in France despite a diet that includes plenty of butter and cheese has come to be known as the French paradox. Some experts have suggested that red wine makes the difference, something the red wine industry has heavily and heartily endorsed. But there's far more to the French paradox than red wine.

The diet and lifestyle in parts of France, especially the south, have much in common with other Mediterranean regions, and these may account for some of the protection against heart disease.

Some studies have suggested that red wine—especially when drunk with a meal—offers more cardiovascular benefits than beer or spirits. These range from international comparisons showing a lower prevalence of coronary heart disease in "wine-drinking countries" than in beer- or liquor-drinking countries.[18-19]

Red wine may contain more and more various substances, in addition to alcohol that may prevent blood clots, relax blood vessel walls, and prevent the oxidation of low-density lipoprotein (LDL, "bad" cholesterol), a key early step in the formation of cholestrol-filled plaque.

In practice, though, beverage choice appears to have little effect on cardiovascular benefit. A report from the Health Professionals Follow-Up Study, for example, examined the drinking habits of more than 38,000 men over a 12-year period. Moderate drinkers were 30-35% less likely to have had a heart attack than non-drinkers.[20]

This reduction was observed among men who drank wine, beer, or spirits, and was similar for those who drank with meals and those who drank outside of meal time. Men who drank every day had a lower risk of heart attack than those who drank once or twice a week.

Notes

1. 10th Annual Report to the U.S. Congress on Alcohol and Health. *National Institute on Alcohol Abuse and Alcoholism.* Washingon, DC, 2000.
2. Dufour, MC. *What Is Moderate Drinking? Defining "Drinks" and Drinking Levels.* Alcohol Res Health 1999; 23: 5–14.
3. Dietary Guidelines for Americans. *U.S. Department of Agriculture, U.S. Department of Health and Human Services. Accessed on 12 March 2003.*
4. Goldberg, IJ, Mosca, L, Piano, MR, Fisher, EA. AHA Science Advisory: Wine and Your Heart: A Science Advisory for Healthcare Professionals from the Nutrition Committee, Council on Epidemiology and Prevention, and Council on Cardiovascular Nursing of the American Heart Association. *Circulation* 2001; 103: 472–5.
5. Ajana, U., Hennekens, C, Spelsberg, A, Manson, JE. Alcohol Consumption and Risk of Type 2 Diabetes Mellitus Among U.S. Male Physicians. *Arch Intern Med* 2000; 160: 1025–30.
6. Camargo, C., Jr., Stampfer, MJ, Glynn, RJ, et al. Prospective Study of Moderate Alcohol Consumption and Risk of Peripheral Arterial Disease in U.S. Male Physicians. *Circulation* 1997; 95: 577–80.
7. Camargo, CA Jr., Stampfer, MJ, Glynn, RJ, et al. Moderate Alcohol Consumption and Risk for Angina Pectoris or Myocardial Infarction in U.S. Male Physicians. *Ann Intern Med* 1997; 126: 372–5.

8. Malinkski, MK, Sesso, HD, Lopez-Jimenez, F, Buring, JM. Alcohol Consumption and Cardiovascular Disease Mortality in Hypertensive Men. *Arch Intern Med* 2004; 164: 623–8.

9. Rimm, EB, Williams, P, Fosher, K, Criqui, M, Stampfer, MJ. Moderate Alcohol Intake and Lower Risk of Coronary Heart Disease: Meta-analysis of Effects on Lipids and Haemostatic Factors. *BMJ* 1999; 319: 1523–8.

10. Dufour, MC. Risks and Benefits of Alcohol Use Over the Life Span. *Alcohol Health and Research World* 1996; 20: 145–51.

11. Leitzmann, MF, Giovannucci, EL, Stampfer, MJ, et al. Prospective Study of Alcohol Consumption Patterns in Relations to Symptomatic Gallstone Disease. *Alcohol Clin Exp Res* 1999; 23: 835–41.

12. Conigrave, KM, Hu, BF, Camargo, CA Jr., Stampfer, MJ, Willett, WC, Rimm, EB. A Prospective Study of Drinking Patterns in Relation to Risk of Type 2 Diabetes Among Men. *Diabetes* 2001; 50: 2390–5.

13. Grodstein, F, Colditz, GA, Hunter, DJ, Manson, JE, Willet, WC, Stampfer, MJ. A Prospective Study of Symptomatic Gallstones in Women: Relation with Oral Contraceptives and Other Risk Factors. *Obstet Gynecol* 1994; 84: 207–14.

14. Chen, WY, Colditz, GA, Rosner, B, et al. Use of Postmenopausal Hormones, Alcohol, and Risk for Invasive Breast Cancer. *Ann Intern Med* 2002; 137: 798–804.

15. Zhang, S, Hunter, DJ, Hankinson, SE, et al. A Prospective Study of Folate Intake and the Risk of Breast Cancer. *JAMA* 1999; 281: 1632–37.

16. Hines, LM, Stampfer, MJ, Ma, J., et al. Genetic Variation in Alcohol Dehydrogenase and the Benefitial Effect of Moderate Alcohol Consumption on Myocardial Infarction. *N Engl J Med*

17. Black, S. 1918. ed. New York: Alex Wilkinson, Clinical and Pathological Reports.

18. St. Leger, AS, Cochraned, AL, Moore, F. Factors Associated with Cardiac Mortality in Developed Countries with Particular Reference to the Consumption of Wine. *Lancet* 1979; 1: 1017–20.

19. Rimm, EB, Klatsky, A, Grobbee, D. Stampfer, MJ. Review of Moderate Alcohol Consumption an Reduced Risk of Coronary Heart Disease: Is the Effect Due to Beer, Wine, or Spirits. *BMJ* 1996; 312: 731–6.

20. Mukamal, KJ, Conigrave, KM, Mittleman, MA, et al. Roles of Drinking Pattern and Type of Alcohol Consumed in Coronary Heart Disease in Men. *N Engl J Med* 2003; 348: 109–18.

21. Zhang, S, Hunter, DJ, Hankinson, SE, et al. Plasma Folate, Vitamin B(6), Vitamin B(12), Homocysteine, and Risk of Breast Cancer. *J Natl Cancer Inst* 2003; 95: 373–80.

22. Zhang, S, Hunter, DJ, Hankinson, SE, et al. A Prospective Study of Folate Intake and the Risk of Breast Cancer. *JAMA* 1999; 281: 1632–7.

23. Klatsky, AL, Armstrong, MA, Friedman, GD. Risk of Cardiovascular Mortality in Alcohol Drinkers, Ex-drinkers, and NonDrinkers. *Am J Cardiol* 1990; 66: 1237–42.

24. Fuchs, CS, Stampfer, MJ, Colditz, GA, et al. Alcohol Consumption and Mortality Among Women. *N Engl Med J* 1995; 332: 1245–50.

25. Stampfer, MJ, Colditz, GA, Willet, WC, Speizer, FE, Hennekens, CH. A Prospective Study of Moderate Alcohol Consumption and the Risk of Coronary Disease and Stroke in Women. *N Engl J Med* 1988; 319: 267–73.

26. Camargo, CA Jr., Hennekens, CH, Gaziano, JM, Glynn, RJ, Manson, JE, Stampfer, MJ. Prospective Study of Moderate Alcohol Consumption and Mortality in U.S. Male Physicians. *Arch Intern Med* 1997; 157: 79–85.
27. Thun, MJ, Petro, R, Lopez, AD, et al. Alcohol Consumption and Mortality Among Middle-aged and Elderly U.S. Adults. *N Engl Med* 1997; 337: 1705–14.
28. Renaud, SC, Gueguen, R, Schenker, J. d'Houtaud, A. Alcohol and Mortality in Middle-aged Men from Eastern France. *Epidemiology* 1998; 9: 184–8.

Appendix

Facts About Alcohol

Alcohol is the most popular drug in the world.

Although "alcohol" is often used to mean alcoholic drinks, it actually refers to a class of chemical substances that contain bonded atoms of carbon, hydrogen, and oxygen. There are several kinds of alcohol, many highly toxic, used for various purposes.

Ethyl alcohol, also called ethanol, is the alcohol found in liquors. It is also used in lacquers, varnishes, stains, detergents, fragrances, flavorings, in gasoline as an additive, and as fuel for specially designed cars.

Ethanol is produced through fermentation, in which yeast breaks down sugar from malted grains, fruits, or other food and turns it into ethyl alcohol and carbon dioxide gas. Grains are used to make beer. Grape or other juice is used to make wine. Sugar from honey will produce mead. Rice is used to make sake, a Japanese wine.

Alcoholic beverages have played a major role in almost all human cultures throughout history.

In all cultures, drinking behavior is regulated, in terms of who may drink, how much, and under what circumstances. These regulations are usually highly controversial.

Agriculture, seen as the foundation of civilization, was developed to grow grain, probably for use in making beer as much as for making bread.

A poem to the Sumerian goddess of brewing, which contains one of the most ancient recipes for beer, was found on a clay tablet dating from 1800 B.C.

"Brewing" is the term used for making drinks such as lager beer and ale. It consists of six steps: malting, mashing, boiling, fermenting, aging, and finishing.

Commercial brewing began on a large-scale basis in Germany in the 1100s. The first brewery in North America was established in 1632 in what is now New York City.

Fermented drinks, such as wine and beer, contain from less than five percent to twenty percent ethyl alcohol.

Hard liquor, also called spirits, is produced by distillation, in which fermented material is heated in a "still" into vapors that are collected and cooled into liquid.

The most popular distilled drinks in the United States include, in order, whiskey, vodka, liqueurs, gin, rum, and brandy.

Alcohol content in distilled liquors is discussed in terms of "proof." In the United States, a liquor's proof is equal to twice the amount of its alcohol content. In other words, if a liquor has forty percent alcohol, it is said to be eighty proof. Most distilled liquors contain from forty percent to fifty percent ethyl alcohol.

Distillation was common as early as 500 B.C. in what is now Pakistan. However, it was probably first used long before then to produce medicine.

Brandy is made from fermented fruit juices; whiskey and vodka from grains such as corn, rye, and wheat; rum from molasses or sugar-cane juice; tequila from maguey (agave) plant juice. For gin, alcohol vapors are blended with flavorings such as juniper berries.

Liqueurs are spirits flavored with leaves, flowers, or fruits, such as apricots, blackberries, and cherries.

The code of Hammurabi, from about 1720 B.C., is among the earliest formal codes restricting excessive drinking. Tavern-keepers, usually women, could be punished with drowning for overcharging and with burning for serving criminals.

A standard drink is one twelve-ounce bottle of beer or wine cooler, one five-ounce glass of wine, or 1.5 ounces of eighty-proof distilled liquor.

Driving skills can be impaired with a blood alcohol level as low as 0.02 percent, lower than most legal limits.

A man weighing 160 pounds (72.5kg) will have a blood alcohol level of 0.04 one hour after drinking two beers on an empty stomach.

More than 150 medications, including acetaminophen (Tylenol) and antihistamines (cold and allergy medicines), can have adverse effects if alcohol is taken while they are in the body.

Alcohol is a risk factor for many cancers. The U.S. National Toxicology Program and the International Agency for Research on Cancer list it as a known human carcinogen.

The human body makes its own alcohol naturally, continuously every day. People always have alcohol in their bodies.

The only cure for alcohol intoxication is time. Common treatments such as black coffee, cold showers, and exercise do not work.

Even though people who drink alcohol often seem stimulated, alcohol depresses the central nervous system. The main effect of alcohol is to slow brain activity.

Chronology

B.C.

3000

Alcoholic drinks are discovered by accident when airborne yeasts cause fermentation in mixtures of fruits, grains, or honey exposed to warm air.

Taverns catering to travelers' appear, beginning trade in alcohol.

2100

Beer, and possibly wine, are used as the main vehicle to administer medicines.

1750

The Code of Hammurabi establishes regulations over pricing and measuring alcohol and prohibiting disorderly gatherings.

1200

The Hebrews, led by Moses out of slavery, regret leaving the wines of Egypt but find abundant vineyards in Palestine.

900

The Rechabites dissent from the growing sophistication of the Hebrews by advocating simplicity and abstaining from, among many things, the use of alcoholic drinks.

625

The worship of the wine god Bacchos Bromios spreads to Greece and becomes associated with Dionysus, a minor Greek god of wine and corn who comes to be worshipped as a son of god. Rituals include ecstatic rites using music, dancing, sacrifice, and drunkenness.

The citizens of the Greek city-state of Sparta become among the most temperate drinkers in the ancient world when wine drinking is allowed only for relief of thirst, and then only in limited amounts.

400

The physician Hippocrates includes wine as part of the treatment for almost all diseases, yet also describes the adverse affects of the drink.

A.D.

50

Roman drunkenness reaches its highest level and is criticized by writer Petronius in the *Satyricon*.

64

The Christian Gospels teach moderation in drinking. St. Paul's writings address drinking in detail, describing wine as an intrinsically good creation of God but denouncing drunkenness.

450

Roman physician Cassius Felix describes symptoms of alcoholism-induced delirium tremens.

500

Arabs develop distilled alcohol.

1050

The medical school in Salerno, Italy, prescribes wine as one of the most frequent therapeutic treatments, but warns against drinking between meals or at the start of a meal.

1200

Beer makers introduce the use of hops, giving beer a stronger taste, a clearer appearance, and acting as a preservative.

1275

Franciscan friar Raymond Lull, an alchemist who spent time among Muslims and spoke Arabic, introduces distilled alcohol to Europe.

1350–1550

After the devastating European plague epidemics of the 1300s, the population experiences an increase in living standards accompanied by increases in both drinking and drunkenness.

1500s–1600s

Distilled spirits appear in Russia for the first time. During the course of the sixteenth century, they come to be known as vodka, meaning "little water."

William Shakespeare's plays reflect growing concerns over drinking, most obviously in the character Falstaff.

1670

Dom Perignon, the wine steward of the abbey of Hautvillers, France, develops sparkling champagne when he invents the cork stopper.

1700s

The consumption of spirits increases tremendously throughout Europe, marked most prominently by the Gin Craze in London in the first half of the century.

Rum becomes a leading product in the British colonies in America, especially in New England. Taverns in America become the center of community life.

1792–1794

American farmers take part in the Whiskey Rebellion against a tax on domestically produced liquor. Although the rebellion is suppressed, the tax is repealed in 1802.

1800s

Whiskey increases in popularity in America as pioneers find it easier to carry hard liquor made from corn than large amounts of beer and wine. Mountain men introduce liquor to Native Americans through the fur trade, often using it to trick them into unfair bargains.

The temperance movement begins in the United States, promoting moderate alcohol use. Due to the heavy drinking habits of Americans, the movement later changes its goals and calls for total abstinence.

1869

The Prohibition Party forms in the United States.

1920

Prohibition becomes an official amendment to the United States Constitution, banning the commercial production and sale of alcohol.

1932

Prohibition is repealed from the United States Constitution.

1935

Alcoholics Anonymous (AA), a self-help group for alcoholics, is created by William Wilson and Robert Smith.

1970s

American states reduce the minimum drinking age to eighteen to match the new voting age; the move soon results in a dramatic rise in alcohol-related traffic accidents.

1973

Fetal alcohol syndrome, a group of central nervous system disorders affecting infants of mothers who use alcohol during pregnancy, is first described in scientific literature in the United States.

1980

Candy Lightner, whose daughter was killed by a drunk driver, forms the organization Mothers Against Drunk Driving (MADD) in Sacramento, California. It becomes a national organization in 1981.

1984

The United States government enacts the Uniform Drinking Age Act, withholding federal highway funds from states with a minimum legal drinking age lower than twenty-one. By 1988, all states have set the legal drinking age at twenty-one.

1990s

Several large studies from many different countries find that people who drink moderate amounts of alcohol have a significantly lower incidence of heart disease.

2006

A study published in the *Archives of Pediatrics and Adolescent Medicine* concludes that exposure to alcohol advertising leads to increased drinking among underage youth.

Organizations to Contact

Al-Anon Family Group Headquarters
1600 Corporate Landing Pkwy.
Virginia Beach, VA   23454-5617
(757) 563-1600 • fax: (757) 563-1655

Capital Corporate Centre
9 Antares Dr., Suite 245, Ottawa, ON
  K2E 7V5
  CANADA
Tel: (613) 723-8484 • fax: (613) 723-0151
E-mail (Canada and U.S.): wso@al-anon.org
Web site: www.al/anon.alateen.org

Al-Anon is a fellowship of people, including children and teens, whose lives have been affected by an alcoholic family member or friend. Members share their experiences, strength, and hope to help each other and perhaps to aid in the recovery of the alcoholic. Al-Anon Family Group Headquarters provides information on its local chapters and on its affiliated organization, Alateen. Its publications include the monthly magazine the *Forum*, several pamphlets, service materials, complimentary literature given to newcomers, and several books, including *Alateen: Hope for Children of Alcoholics, One Day at a Time in Al-Anon, The Al-Anon Family Groups Classic Edition*, and *Al-Anon's Twelve Steps & Twelve Traditions*.

Alcohol Advisory Council of New Zealand
Level 13, Castrol House, 36 Customhouse Quay
PO Box 5023,, Wellington
  New Zealand
Phone: 04-917-0600 • fax: 04-473-0890
e-mail: central@alac.org.nz
Web site: www.alcohol.org.nz

The Alcohol Advisory Council of New Zealand's primary objective is to promote moderation in the use of alcohol and develop and promote strategies that will reduce alcohol problems for the nation. ALAC has a Maori Unit that coordinates culturally appropriate initiatives to reduce alcohol-related harm for the Maori. The organization publishes a quarterly newsletter in addition to research reports and government studies. All publications are available on its Web site.

Alcoholics Anonymous (AA)
General Service Office, PO Box 459
Grand Central Station, New York, NY   10163
(212) 870-3400 • fax: (212) 870-3003
Web site: http://www.alcoholics-anonymous.org/

Alcoholics Anonymous is an international fellowship of men and women who are recovering from alcoholism. Because AA's primary goal is to help alcoholics remain sober, it does not sponsor research or engage in education about alcoholism. AA does, however, publish a catalog of literature concerning the organization as well as several pamphlets, which are available through the General Service Office or local groups that can be found on the general Web site.

American Beverage Institute (ABI)
1775 Pennsylvania Ave. NW, Suite 1200
Washington, DC   20006
(202) 463-7110
Web site: www.abionline.org

The American Beverage Institute is a restaurant industry trade organization that works to protect the responsible consumption of alcoholic beverages in the restaurant setting. It unites the wine, beer, and spirits producers with distributors and on-premise retailers in this effort. It conducts research and education in an attempt to demonstrate that the vast majority of adults who drink alcohol outside of the home are responsible, law-abiding citizens. Its Web site includes fact sheets and news articles on various issues, such as the American Beverage Institute's Server Training Program Certification program to help the hospitality industry prevent irresponsible drinking, and research reports including "The Anti-Drunk Driving Campaign: A Covert War Against Drinking" and "The .08 Debate: What's the Harm?"

American Society of Addiction Medicine (ASAM)
4601 N. Park Ave., Upper Arcade #101
Chevy Chase, MD 20815
(301) 656-3920 • fax: (301) 656-3815
e-mail: email@asam.org
Web site: www.asam.org

ASAM is the nation's addiction medicine specialty society dedicated to educating physicians and improving the treatment of individuals suffering from alcoholism and other addictions. In addition, the organization promotes research and prevention of addiction and works for the establishment of addiction medicine as a specialty recognized by the American Board of Medical Specialties. The organization publishes medical texts and a bimonthly newsletter.

The Beer Institute
122 C St. NW, Suite 750, Washington, DC 20001
(202) 737-2337
e-mail: info@beerinstitute.org
Web site: www.beerinstitute.org

The Beer Institute is a trade organization that represents the beer industry before Congress, state legislatures, and public forums across the country. It sponsors educational programs to prevent underage drinking and drunk driving and distributes fact sheets and news briefs on issues such as alcohol taxes and advertising.

Canadian Centre on Substance Abuse/Centre canadien de lutte contre l'alcoolisme et les toxicomanies (CCSA/CCLAT)

75 Albert St., Suite 300, Ottawa, ON
K1P 5E7 CANADA
(613) 235-4048 • fax: (613) 235-8101
e-mail: info@ccsa.ca
Web site: www.ccsa.ca

A Canadian clearinghouse on substance abuse, the CCSA/CCLAT works to disseminate information on the nature, extent, and consequences of substance abuse and to support and assist organizations involved in substance abuse treatment, prevention, and educational programming. The CCSA/CCLAT publishes several books, including *Canadian Profile: Alcohol, Tobacco, and Other Drugs*, as well as reports, policy documents, brochures, research papers, and the newsletter *Action News*.

Center for Science in the Public Interest (CSPI)

1875 Connecticut Ave. NW, Suite 300
Washington, DC   20009
(202) 332-9110 • fax: (202) 265-4954
e-mail: cspi@cspinet.org
Web site: www.cspinet.org

The center is an advocacy organization that promotes nutrition and health, food safety, alcohol policy, and sound science. It favors the implementation of public policies aimed at reducing alcohol-related problems, such as restricting alcohol advertising and increasing alcohol taxes. CSPI publishes the monthly *Nutrition Action Healthletter*, and its Web site contains fact sheets and reports on alcohol-related problems and alcohol policies.

Centre for Addiction and Mental Health/Centre de toxicomanie et de santé mentale (CAMH)
33 Russell St., Toronto, ON
M5S 2S1
CANADA
(416) 535-8501
Web site: www.camh.net

CAMH is a public hospital and the largest addiction facility in Canada. It also functions as a research facility, an education and training center, and a community-based organization providing health and addiction prevention services throughout Ontario, Canada. Further, CAMH is fully affiliated with the University of Toronto and is a Pan American Health Organization and World Health Organization Collaborating Centre. CAMH publishes regular newsletters and journals, including the quarterly *CrossCurrents, the Journal of Addiction and Mental Health* and offers free alcoholism prevention literature that can either be downloaded or ordered on its Web site.

Century Council
1310 G St. NW, Suite 600, Washington, DC   20005
(202) 637-0077 • fax: (202) 637-0079
e-mail:kimballl@centurycouncil.org
Web site: www.centurycouncil.org

A nonprofit organization funded by America's liquor industry, the Century Council's mission is to fight drunk driving and underage drinking. It seeks to promote responsible decision making about drinking and discourage all forms of irresponsible alcohol consumption through education, communications, research, law enforcement, and other programs. Its Web site offers fact sheets and other resources on drunk driving, underage drinking, and other alcohol-related problems.

Distilled Spirits Council of the United States (DISCUS)
1250 Eye St. NW, Suite 900, Washington, DC   20005

(202) 628-3544
Web site: www.discus.org

The Distilled Spirits Council of the United States is the national trade association representing producers and marketers of distilled spirits in the United States. It seeks to ensure the responsible advertising and marketing of distilled spirits to adult consumers and to prevent such advertising and marketing from targeting individuals below the legal purchase age. DISCUS publishes fact sheets, news releases, and documents, including its "Code of Responsible Practices for Beverage Alcohol Advertising and Marketing."

International Center for Alcohol Policies (ICAP)
1519 New Hampshire Ave. NW, Washington, DC   20036
(202) 986-1159 • fax: (202) 986-2080
Web site: www.icap.org

The International Center for Alcohol Policies is a nonprofit organization dedicated to helping reduce the abuse of alcohol worldwide and to promote understanding of the role of alcohol in society through dialogue and partnerships involving the beverage industry, the public health community, and others interested in alcohol policy. ICAP is supported by major international alcoholic beverage companies. ICAP publishes several books, including the Series on Alcohol and Society, intended to promote a fresh and more balanced perspective on a key alcohol policy issue, and also reports on pertinent issues such as *Alcohol Education and Its Effectiveness, Drinking Patterns: From Theory to Practice,* and *Alcohol and the Workplace.*

The Marin Institute
24 Belvedere St., San Rafael, CA   94901
(415) 456-5692 • fax (415) 456-0491
e-mail: info@marininstitute.org
Web site: www.marininstitute.org

The Marin Institute is an alcohol industry watchdog organization that works to protect the public from the impact of the alcohol industry's practices. It works to reduce alcohol problems through environmental prevention—improving the physical and social environment to promote health and safety. The institute promotes stricter alcohol policies—including higher taxes—in order to reduce alcohol-related problems. It publishes fact sheets and news alerts on alcohol policy, advertising, and other alcohol-related issues. Its "Talk Back System" allows users of its Web site to complain directly to the alcohol industry about irresponsible advertising and marketing practices.

Mothers Against Drunk Driving (MADD)
511 E. John Carpenter Frwy., Suite 700, Irving, TX   75062
800-GET-MADD (438-6233) • fax: (972) 869-2206/07
Web site: www.madd.org

Mothers Against Drunk Driving seeks to stop drunk driving, prevent underage drinking, and support victims of drunk-driving accidents by speaking on their behalf to communities, businesses, and educational groups and by providing materials for use in medical facilities and health and driver's education programs. MADD publishes the biannual *MADDvocate for Victims Magazine* as well as a variety of fact sheets, brochures, and other materials on drunk driving.

National Center on Addiction and Substance Abuse (CASA)
633 Third Ave., 19th Floor, New York, NY   10017-6706
Phone: (212) 841-5200 • fax: (212) 956-8020
Web site: www.casacolumbia.org

CASA is a nonprofit organization affiliated with Columbia University. It works to educate the public about the problems of substance abuse and addiction and to evaluate prevention, treatment, and law enforcement programs to address the problem. Its Web site contains reports and articles on alcohol policy and the alcohol industry, including the reports *'You've Got Drugs!' Prescription Drug Pushers on the Internet* and *The Commercial Value of Underage and Pathological Drinking to the Alcohol Industry.*

National Council on Alcoholism and Drug Dependence (NCADD)

22 Cortlandt St., Suite 801, New York, NY 10007-3128
Phone: (212) 269-7797 • fax: (212) 269-7510
e-mail: national@ncadd.org
Web site: www.ncadd.org

NCADD is a volunteer health organization that helps individuals overcome addictions, advises the federal government on drug and alcohol policies, and develops substance abuse prevention and education programs for youth. It publishes brochures such as *Who's Got the Power? You . . . or Drugs?*, fact sheets such as *Youth, Alcohol and Other Drugs*, and the booklet, *Ask Dr. Bob: Questions and Answers on Alcoholism.*

National Highway Traffic Safety Administration (NHTSA)

400 Seventh St., SW, Washington, DC 20590
(888) 327-4236
http://www.nhtsa.dot.gov

The NHTSA is a department of the U.S. Department of Transportation that is responsible for reducing deaths, injuries, and economic losses resulting from motor vehicle crashes. It sets and enforces safety performance standards for motor vehicles and motor vehicle equipment and awards grants to state and local governments to enable them to conduct local highway safety programs. The NHTSA publishes information on drunk driving, including *Get the Keys* and *Strategies for Success: Combating Juvenile DUI.*

National Institute on Alcoholism and Alcohol Abuse (NIAAA)

5635 Fishers La., MSC 9304, Bethesda, MD   20892-9304
email: niaaaweb-r@exchange.nih.gov
Web site: www.niaaa.nih.gov

The National Institute on Alcoholism and Alcohol Abuse is one of the eighteen institutes that compose the National Institutes of Health. NIAAA provides leadership in the national effort to reduce alcohol-related problems. NIAAA is an excellent source of information and publishes the quarterly bulletin, *Alcohol Alert*; a quarterly scientific journal, *Alcohol Research and Health*; and many pamphlets, brochures, and posters dealing with alcohol abuse and alcoholism. All of these publications as well as answers to frequently asked questions about alcohol, including NIAAA's congressional testimony, are available online.

National Organization on Fetal Alcohol Syndrome (NOFAS)

900 Seventeenth St. NW, Suite 910, Washington, DC   20006
(202) 785-4585 • fax: (202) 466-6456
Web site: www.nofas.org

NOFAS is a nonprofit organization dedicated to eliminating birth defects caused by alcohol consumption during pregnancy and to improving the quality of life for those individuals and families affected. The organization sponsors many outreach and educational programs and publishes a quarterly newsletter, *Notes from NOFAS*, in addition to many fact sheets and brochures. Some information is available online. An information packet can be ordered through the mail.

Rational Recovery Systems (RRS)

PO Box 800, Lotus, CA   95651
(530) 621-2667
e-mail: rrsn@rational.org
Web site: www.rational.org/recovery

RRS is a national self-help organization that offers a cognitive rather than spiritual approach (like AA) to recovery from alcoholism. Its philosophy holds that alcoholics can attain sobriety without depending on other people or a "higher power." Rational Recovery Systems publishes materials about the organization and its use of rational-emotive therapy.

Research Society on Alcoholism (RSA)
7801 N. Lamar Blvd., Suite D-89, Austin, TX   78752-1038
(512) 454-0022 • fax: (512) 454-0812
e-mail: DebbyRSA@sbcglobal.net
Web site: www.rsoa.org

The RSA provides a forum for researchers who share common interests in alcoholism. The society's purpose is to promote research on the prevention and treatment of alcoholism. It publishes the journal *Alcoholism: Clinical and Experimental Research* nine times a year as well as the book series *Recent Advances in Alcoholism.*

Secular Organizations for Sobriety (SOS)
4773 Hollywood Blvd., Hollywood, CA   90027
Phone: (323) 666-4295 • fax: (323) 666-4271
e-mail: sos@cfiwest.org
Web site: www.secularsobriety.org

SOS is a network of groups dedicated to helping individuals achieve and maintain sobriety. The organization believes that alcoholics can best recover by rationally choosing to make sobriety rather than alcohol a priority. Most members of SOS reject the spiritual basis of Alcoholics Anonymous and other similar self-help groups. SOS publishes the quarterly *SOS International Newsletter* and distributes several books, including *Unhooked: Staying Sober and Drug Free* and *How to Stay Sober: Recovery Without Religion*, and *SOS Sobriety: The Proven Alternative to 12-Step Programs*, written by SOS founder James Christopher.

Substance Abuse and Mental Health
Services Administration (SAMSA)
PO Box 2345, Rockville, MD   20852
Phone: (800) 729-6686; (301) 468-2600 • fax: (301) 468-6433
Web site: www.health.org

SAMSA is a division of the U.S. Department of Health and Human Services that is responsible for improving the lives of those with or at risk for mental illness or substance addiction. Through the NCADI, SAMSA provides the public with a wide variety of information on alcoholism and other addictions. Its publications include newsletters, the fact sheet *Alcohol Alert*, research monographs, brochures, pamphlets, videotapes, and posters. Publications and telephone advice in Spanish are also available.

For Further Research

Books

Alcoholics Anonymous, *The Story of How Many Thousands of Men and Women Have Recovered from Alcoholism.* 3rd ed. New York: Alcoholics Anonymous World Services, 1976.

Percy Andreae, *The Prohibition Movement in its Broader Bearings upon our Social, Commercial, and Religious Liberties.* Chicago: Felix Mendelsohn, 1915.

Karen F. Balkin, *Alcohol: Opposing Viewpoints.* San Diego: Greenhaven, 2004.

Susanna Barrows and Robin Room, *Drinking: Behavior and Belief in Modern History.* Berkeley and Los Angeles: University of California Press, 1991.

Eric Burns, *The Spirits of America: A Social History of Alcohol.* Philadelphia: Temple University Press, 2004.

Susan and Daniel Cohen, *A Six-Pack and a Fake I.D.: Teens Look at the Drinking Question.* New York: Dell, 1992.

Griffith Edwards, *Alcohol: The World's Favorite Drug.* New York: Thomas Dunne/St. Martin's, 2002.

David J. Hanson, *Preventing Alcohol Abuse: Alcohol, Culture, and Control.* Westport, CT: Praeger, 1995.

HaiSong Harvey, *Alcohol Abuse.* San Diego: Greenhaven, 2003.

David E. Kyvig, *Repealing National Prohibition.* Kent, OH: Kent State University Press, 2000.

Ian Macdonald, *Health Issues Related to Alcohol Consumption.* 2nd ed. Oxford, UK: International Life Sciences Institute, 1999.

Hank Nuwer, *Wrongs of Passage: Fraternities, Sororities, Hazing, and Binge Drinking*. Bloomington: Indiana University Press, 1999.

Auriana Ojeda, *Teens at Risk: Opposing Viewpoints*. San Diego: Greenhaven, 2003.

Robert Nash Parker, *Alcohol and Homicide: A Deadly Combination of Two American Traditions*. Albany: State University of New York Press, 1995.

J. Vincent Peterson, Bernard Nisenholz, and Gary Robinson, *A Nation Under the Influence: America's Addiction to Alcohol*. Boston: Pearson Education, 2003.

Upton Sinclair, *The Cup of Fury*. Manhasset, NY: Channel, 1956.

Jessica Warner, *Craze: Gin and Debauchery in an Age of Reason*. New York: Four Walls Eight Windows, 2002.

Henry Wechsler and Bernice Wuethrich, *Dying to Drink: Confronting Binge Drinking on College Campuses*. Emmaus, PA: Rodale, 2002.

Periodicals

Jim Adams, "Teens and Alcohol: Underage Drinking Is a Big Problem in the U.S.; Many Teens Don't Know What Drinking Can Do to Them," *Junior Scholastic*, February 11, 2002.

William F. Allman, "Until a Cure Is Found: Science and the Five-Star Hangover," *Forbes*, November 18, 1996.

Virginia Berridge, "Why Alcohol Is Legal and Other Drugs Are Not," *History Today*, May 2004.

John C. Crabbe, David Goldman, "Alcoholism: A Complex Genetic Disease," *Alcohol Health & Research World*, Fall 1992.

Shirley Dang, "Breathalyzer Debate Returns," *Contra Costa (CA) Times*, November 6, 2005.

Hank Grezlak, "Does DUI Stop Signal 'Police State'?" *Legal Intelligencer*, March 28, 2005.

Nicole LaFreniere and Jessica Kowal, "I Drove Drunk and Killed Three People," *Cosmopolitan*, January 2005.

Lancet, "Time for Coordinated Action on Alcohol," March 27, 2004.

John de Miranda, "We Must Move from Disease Concept to Disability Model," *Alcoholism & Drug Abuse Weekly*, September 24, 2001.

Michele Oreckin, "You Must Be over 21 to Drink in This Living Room: A Crackdown on House Parties Stirs Up a Debate About Privacy," *Time*, April 18, 2005.

Charlotte Raven, "Drink and Be Damned: New Laws Won't Reduce our Frantic Consumption of Alcohol," *New Statesman*, February 7, 2005.

Henry Saffer, "Alcohol Advertising and Youth," *Journal of Studies on Alcohol*, March 2002.

Richard Saitz, "Introduction to Alcohol Withdrawal," *Alcohol Health and Research World*, vol. 22, no. 1, 1998.

Bill Schweber, "Take a Deep Breath; Then Exhale Fully: The Breathalyzer Combines Technology, Chemistry, Physiology, and Legality to Make a 'Clear' Assessment of Blood-Alcohol Concentration," *Reed Business Information*, October 16, 2003.

Dinitia Smith, "A Serious Business for a Humorous Drunkard," *New York Times*, October 30, 2004.

Steven R. Thomsen and Dag Rekve, "The Differential Effects of Exposure to 'Youth-Oriented' Magazines on Adolescent Alcohol Use," *Contemporary Drug Problems*, Spring 2004.

Index